Michela Arturina Betta is an authoress of literature. She was born in Italy where she grew up and went to school. She studied in Milan and Frankfurt where she received her PhD. She worked as an academic in Germany and Australia, Melbourne, and has written essays and books on ethics. Her fascination with literature dates back to her childhood when she won a poetry prize at the age of seven. She now lives in Stockholm. *The Vault of Svalbard* is her latest book. Previous works of fiction are *Stories for Posthuman Readers* and *The Gatekeeper/s*.

Michela Arturina Betta

THE VAULT OF SVALBARD

AUSTIN MACAULEY PUBLISHERS™

LONDON • CAMBRIDGE • NEW YORK • SHARJAH

A CIP catalogue record for this title is available from the British Library.

ISBN 9781398410947 (Paperback)
ISBN 9781398410954 (ePub e-book)

www.austinmacauley.com

First Published 2022
Austin Macauley Publishers Ltd®
1 Canada Square
Canary Wharf
London
E14 5AA

The Principal Characters, Events and Places of the Story

Achilles	Director of the Global Agency for Informed Consent (GAIC) and Top Negotiator of Organisation Number One (ONO)
Adam Featherstone	Computer and A.I. expert; Member of the GAIC scientific team
Ajana, Emily, Fatim, Luca,	The four interns at GAIC
Åke Mio	Professor of Unusuality
Albert Melitus	Professor of Water
Amastan Badis	Husband of Queen Gwafa Illi Tin
Hammadit	Hinan and Rector of the University of the Desert
Angelo Tudor	Achilles' personal assistant and GAIC's Secretary
Annabelle	Junior secretary at GAIC; reports to Achilles
CA	Complex algorithm
Carlos, Juanita, Manolo, Pablo, Rosetta, Senorita	Achilles' neighbours
Claire Carlie	Geographer and ecological historian; childhood friend of Achilles

Claus Reverber	Chair of the Nordic Alliance
Colonel Dag Olsen	Military advisor to Achilles
Colonel James Neill	Military advisor to Achilles
The Earth Movement	Environmental and political youth organisation
GAIC	Global Agency for Informed Consent
George Lee	Geologist with expertise in soil and rock formations; Member of GAIC's scientific team
Gwafa Illi Tin Hinan	Queen of the Tuaregs (the Blue People); Owner of the University of the Desert and Head of the Blue City
IBEFR	Industrial Business Economic Financial Representation
Informed Consent	ONO's doctrine of governance
John Delafort	Archaeologist; married to Claire Carlie
Justin Goldbrain	Professor of infectious diseases
Longyearbyen Military Base	Norway
Lucillo	Junior secretary at GAIC; reports to Achilles
Marie-Louise Goldbrain	Professor of infectious diseases
Martha White	Marine biologist and ocean physicist; Member of GAIC's scientific team
Massachusetts Institute of A.I.	Consultant to Adam Featherstone

Meher Kathri	Geneticist; Member of GAIC's scientific team
Mother	Achilles' mother; lives in the London Residence of Uncle Williams
Mount View University	Consultants to Adam Featherstone
Negotiation	The method of Informed Consent
Nordic Alliance	Denmark, Finland, Germany, Iceland, Norway, Sweden, The Netherlands and the United Kingdom; Member of the International Alliance for Agricultural Heritage
NU	Nations United (replaced by ONO)
ONO	Organisation Number One
Parys	Junior secretary at GAIC; reports to Achilles
Roman Lutowsky	Civil engineer and expert in natural materials and construction material; Member of GAIC's scientific team
Romeo	GAIC's chef and Achilles' confidant
Save the Earth	Music band and the public face of the Earth Movement
Soldiers	Asbjørn Larsen, Bente Hansen and Daniel Sandvig; report to Colonel Dag Olsen
The Negotiators	Tasked with presiding negotiations; report to Achilles
The Rhetoricians	Tasked with leading negotiations to achieve informed consent; report to Achilles

Uncle William	Consultant to the British Government; Achilles' uncle
Vault of Svalbard	A fictitious place in Longyearbyen, Norway

Chapter 1

Achilles arrived in Oslo at noon. Since his promotion to the top negotiator of Organisation Number One, also known as ONO, it had been his ambition to visit governments on a regular basis. His main objective in doing so was to monitor the introduction of informed consent into the legal frameworks of all ONO members. Informed consent was ONO's doctrine and the Global Agency for Informed Consent, also known as GAIC, was responsible for the establishment, promotion and enforcement of informed consent through negotiation. Achilles was GAIC's director.

As his meeting with the representatives of the Norwegian government was scheduled for the afternoon, Achilles decided to pay a visit to the Munch Museum. He was about to enter it when Angelo called him.

"Sir…" From the tone of voice of his personal assistant Achilles could perceive a sense of urgency.

"Yes!"

"The vault, sir, the vault has been robbed."

"Which vault?" It seemed impossible to him that Angelo was speaking of the global seed vault in Longyearbyen.

"Sir, the vault of Svalbard has been vandalised. Seeds have been stolen and…"

"Impossible!" Achilles interrupted him.

As Angelo did not react, Achilles understood the enormity of the situation.

"When did it happen?"

"Not sure."

"I can't believe it!" Again Achilles expressed his surprise. "The Norwegian government had promised top-level security," he added. He was right. Everyone considered the Svalbard vault to be impregnable but now it turned out that it was not. Achilles heard background noises and concluded that people must be standing in Angelo's office awaiting his instructions. But he needed time to think about the news he had just received before advising his aides.

"Thank you, Angelo. I'll get back to you from my hotel room." Achilles was about to close off the conversation when he felt hesitant.

"Tell me, who brought the news?"

"An anonymous message was sent to one of your work devices."

"Hm."

"Sir?"

"It could be a prank!"

"The message includes an image which shows the door of the vault... totally open. There is also a broken bag full of seeds on the ground, more seeds scattered all over the entrance where traces of blood are also visible." Angelo's voice trembled.

"Blood?"

The vault of Svalbard was one of humanity's most important projects; accordingly, when it was inaugurated it raised great expectations. The vault was established by the Nordic Alliance that included Denmark, Finland, Germany, Iceland, Norway, Sweden, The Netherlands and the United Kingdom. The Nordic Alliance was a member of the International Alliance for Agricultural Heritage, an umbrella institution that focused on fundraising by mainly seeking public grants and private money for its agricultural projects. Some of these projects encompassed the maintenance of regional seed banks, particularly the Svalbard vault that was the most prestigious of all the seed banks. The Svalbard enterprise enjoyed the support of fifty governments and eighty research institutes worldwide. The Nordic Alliance had given The Global Seeds and Plant Diversity Trust the task to collect and manage the seeds. To confer on the vault the global importance it deserved, ONO became the ultimate legal guarantor of the project.

Initially, though, that responsibility rested with Nations United (NU) but a few years after the opening of the seed vault, ONO replaced NU. As a result, ONO became the new legal guarantor of the vault of Svalbard. Created to boost international cooperation after the tumultuous times that followed the two world wars, NU failed to live up to its own principles and seldom achieved its own goals. Its replacement signalled a new start in global cooperation. ONO took over the policies related to safety and security originally initiated by NU. One of these policies covered the Doomsday vault, as the vault of Svalbard was affectionately called by many.

The clause concerning the ultimate legal guarantor was always seen as a pure formality. No one, really, expected it to be ever invoked in matters related to the vault, thus its importance was underestimated. In reality, however, the clause granted wide-ranging powers. It established that in case of extraordinary events with global repercussions the legal guarantor would automatically become the ultimate owner of the entire internal space of the vault and its content. Which was a lot. In the first ten years of operations, more than one million seeds were stored in the vault of Svalbard, with many more added in the years that followed. The vault was now the custodian of some very precious material for it was generally believed that those tiny things represented the agricultural inventiveness of nearly 15,000 years of human history.

Chapter 2

Achilles called Bjarne, the owner of the hotel where he was going to stay while he was in Oslo to advise him of his earlier arrival. He and Bjarne had been friends since their university studies. Their friendship was genuine, and when they met, which in fact did not happen very often due to Achilles' work, they enjoyed every minute together.

"I only have time for a quick drink," Achilles said to Bjarne when he entered the hotel where his friend was waiting for him. "Troubles!"

They spoke briefly about his trip while sipping a warm coffee before Achilles retired to his suite. From here, he immediately called his personal assistant Angelo Tudor, a first-class Latinist and historian, and a descendant of the Tudors. Angelo had studied at Oxford, was known for his proficiency in everything he did and was offered an academic position after the completion of his PhD. Academia had awoken his intellectual passions but also disappointed his expectations turning a promising relationship into a short-lived infatuation. What he despised the most of all things occurring in universities was the lack of ideas and the corrosion of character caused by modern academic life. After leaving university, he went to the Vatican where he worked as one of the three junior secretaries to the Pope. To be at the Vatican had been an amazing experience but he also soon understood that there were personal implications in being involved with the Catholic Church. One day, when he felt particularly strongly that this was not a world he wanted to be part of, he resigned. He left a written note for the Pope, who always remembered him as his best Latinist. Angelo went back to England to write the history of his famous family. After two months, though, he realised that writing was an isolating activity, and isolation was the last thing he needed right now. Increasingly, he wished to be involved with the world and perhaps to work for an organisation that dealt with people's struggles in genuine ways. This is when he thought of GAIC. He had heard a lot about Achilles and his extraordinary success as a negotiator.

Angelo decided to write to him and to offer his services. In his letter, he declared that he was interested in working without pay for a year at the end of which he would consider applying for a position if he still liked the job. On reading Angelo's letter, Achilles gained the impression that Angelo was self-confident, for he seemed to think that any decision concerning his future work with GAIC was basically up to him alone. Achilles decided to meet with him.

"What can you do except for speaking Latin and writing the history of your family?" Achilles asked Angelo while examining him with his inscrutable eyes.

"I can think," Angelo answered without hesitation, "I can think for you when you are too busy so that you can still think for all of us when you are too busy."

Achilles secretly smiled at such a subtle answer. He was sitting with his arms folded, pressing back on his chair as if considering the situation. Then he rose and in stretching out his hand to Angelo, he offered him a position as his personal secretary. He also warned Angelo that he could tell him when work started in the morning but not when it finished.

"In here, the days are long, the nights short."

"Taken," Angelo replied.

The following day when he came to the office, Angelo learned that at GAIC things are done rapidly. Angelo's new office was next to Achilles' and when he entered it he was pleased to find that his new desk had been equipped with the most modern devices. He also noticed several folders left on it along with a handwritten note. "Welcome, Angelo. I look forward to working with you. These three folders contain important documents relating to an imminent negotiation about the granting of new rights to children. Can you please read the background information and summarise it for our next meeting with the relevant agency? You'll find more instructions and documents on your desktop. Happy start, Achilles!"

Another note informed him about his job classification and salary. Angelo felt happy.

"Tell me what you know but be quick," Achilles said hastily when Angelo took his call.

"Our experts seem to suggest that the anonymous message sent to you comes from the Norwegian military."

"Leaked?"

"Yes. It is a long message, to be sure. Actually, it describes how the theft of the seeds was discovered and the inspection of the vault that the military conducted immediately after the discovery."

While they were waiting for the material to be displayed on Achilles' device, Angelo informed him that the DG, as the ONO director-general was nicknamed by his staff, had granted him an hour to check the facts and contact him.

"Thanks, Angelo. I will now read the report and then speak with the DG."

Achilles opened the file. The words 'Top Secret' and 'Classified' written in red ink on the first page revealed the level of importance assigned to it. They also suggested that the person who had leaked the report must have had access to privileged information. Achilles began to read the report and soon discovered that it was written in a style that mixed recounted events with comments.

'During a routine helicopter inspection of the area surrounding the Svalbard vault, a crew of six soldiers noticed a group of polar bears lying on the shore. They immediately landed. Two of the crew left the helicopter and moved close to the animals and saw that the bears had been shot dead. In the meantime, the other four soldiers had informed the Longyearbyen military base about the situation. Colonel Dag Olsen was urgently called to the command room. While they were describing to him what was going on, the crew on the ground heard a loud bang, followed by a second one, which they described to Colonel Olsen as a squawky kind of a sound, similar to when metal grinds against metal. From their position, the two soldiers said, they could only see the right-hand side of the vault and parts of the large entrance. Olsen asked them to move closer to the building to check the status of the main door. As the soldier started to walk toward the vault, they heard another loud bang.

They immediately stopped trying to figure out where the sounds came from but unable to draw any conclusion, they resumed their walk and soon found themselves in front of the vault, a few more steps and they reached the ramp that led to the main entrance. It was then that they saw with horror two polar bears walking in their direction. On noticing the two soldiers, the bears rose on their hind legs, stood in that position for a few seconds and then started running down the ramp. After killing them, the soldiers speedily walked back to the helicopter, and as they did so they saw more bears come out of the vault.

As the ground was slippery, the two soldiers realised that they might not make it safely to the vehicle. Through some kind of survival instinct, they turned to the right into the tiny hall of a small building that stood next to the vault, where the vault's energy battery was kept. The small building was surrounded by a wall which although not very tall was high enough to screen the soldiers from the bears' view. Having lost sight of the two soldiers on the ground, the bears continued to run towards the helicopter and as they approached it, they were shot dead by the other four soldiers. The military people at the base followed the dramatic events on their electronic devices. The two soldiers on the ground returned to the helicopter, and having considered the situation carefully, judged it to be safer not to dispose of the body of the dead animals lying on the shore. This turned out to be a wise decision, for as soon as the helicopter took off more bears were seen walking down the ramp.

The military inspection was led by Captain Asbjørn Larsen; the captain asked Olsen permission to carry out an inspection of the vault before returning to the base.

Permission was granted and as a result, Larsen asked the pilot Bente Hansen to get close to the building. Flying slowly, she approached the entrance of the vault. The soldiers immediately saw that the main door had been blown apart. It was still hooked on the upper door hinge, though, and while it was hanging down, the wind, which was particularly strong on that day, made it hit against the doorjamb causing the metallic noise that the soldiers had described to their colonel. A broken bag containing seeds was visible on the ground. The soldiers took several pictures of the crime scene. They were now flying over the roof and Larsen, in noticing a rope lying on the pavement, decided to take a closer look at it. He asked Hansen to drop as low as possible to allow him to jump on the rooftop. The flat roof of the vault had a metallic construction in the middle. The construction looked like a cube, was 60 inches high and had six open slots connected to each other through three metallic beams.

After a quick assessment, Larsen informed the others that the cube had been damaged and that somebody had forced their entry into the vault by enlarging two of the slots. He also reported that there were two ropes hanging down from one of the beams on the right-hand side of the cube; a third rope, which had caught his attention earlier, had been left rolled up on the ground, despite it being fastened to the beam connecting the two slots on the left-hand side.

Larsen decided to slide down one of the ropes and requested help from two crews. Two soldiers jumped on the roof to help him. On noticing, however, that the vault walls were very high, Daniel Sandvig, one of the two soldiers, asked permission to accompany Larsen. Olsen gave his approval since he reckoned that Sandvig's hiking skills could turn useful during the operation. Larsen and Sandvig now slid down the two ropes hanging next to each other and in this way entered the vault. In the meantime, the helicopter crew had landed next to the building to wait for their return. The waiting soon proved to be nerve-racking.

It took some time before Larsen and Sandvig could reach the floor of the vault. Finally, Larsen's voice was heard. They could not see much, he said, but the room in which they had landed must be quite large since they could not see where it ended despite their headlights. The lack of familiarity with the structure of the vault also made it difficult for them to decide what to do next. Larsen also reported hearing screams but could not tell where they were coming from, although he could definitely say that they were not human screams. After some consideration, it was decided to suspend the present operation and return to Longyearbyen. Once at the military base, the crew recounted the whole event, from the moment they first saw the bodies of the dead bears lying on the shore to their inspection of the vault.

Olsen requested the last three reports about the military visits to the vault. Because inspections to the vault of Svalbard occurred monthly, he explained, it might be helpful to see if anything unusual had been reported but not followed up. To everybody's great surprise, though, only the report from the last visit could be found, which meant that the previous two reports were missing. To add to the dismay caused by the two missing reports, Olsen was also informed that the crews involved in the two undocumented inspections had been discharged, and even more disconcerting, that the same crew had gone to the vault twice. It was established practice that inspecting crews changed every month to avoid having the same crew go more than once a year. How it had come to such a breach of protocol no one could tell, and Olsen expressed his anger in colourful language. He also reassured the interior minister, who had been on video call since the discovery of the dead polar bears, that the military would try to locate the whereabouts of the discharged staff, and that the Norwegian police would be involved in the search. Olsen had joined the base only a month earlier to investigate some irregularities that had compromised security. The colonel suggested that they should share no details about the crisis at the Svalbard vault with other organisations and states for the time being. Especially ONO had to be kept in the dark about the situation until the missing inspection reports were found.'

On this final note, the report ended. Somebody, however, must have disliked the exclusion of ONO and decided to leak it to Achilles. He did not appreciate the colonel's decision and was rendered suspicious of his motives.

"Phew, what a mess!" said Achilles aloud while stretching out in his chair. As he was going through the report in his mind, Achilles found the whole issue atypical. Experience told him that to understand the theft and the vandalism associated with it it might be necessary to adopt an unusual approach. While he was making this point, he recalled having read some time ago about a professor of unusuality who was living in Stockholm. People said that he taught students how to look for the unexpected, the illogical, the improbable and that he had opened a private college for a few selected students, precisely those who did not fit into mainstream universities. To the dismay of traditional academia, however, those who came to him were the best and the brightest, perhaps being unusual and bright was now in fashion.

"Who is this professor?"

"He is called Åke Mio," Angelo replied, "and was a researcher at the Vatican during my time there. Mio was a Latinist who got increasingly interested in artificial intelligence. One day he disappeared and never came back again." After a brief pause Angelo added, in a serious tone, "Åke is a genius and as such he cannot work for others."

"Hm."

"I have lost contact with him but it wouldn't be too difficult for me to find out his access code."

"What else can he do beyond knowing Latin and A.I.?"

"He can understand," Angelo answered as if understanding was something special.

"How is understanding different from thinking?" Achilles asked.

"Well, one can think without understanding what one is thinking about," replied Angelo coolly.

"You can think, he can understand, I wonder what the next person can do."

"Who knows," said Angelo, smiling.

Checking the time, Achilles realised that the director-general might be awaiting his video call and in saying so to Angelo, closed off the conversation.

Chapter 3

"We have a serious problem, Achilles," said the director-general in a calm voice, visibly pleased to see Achilles.

"Tell me what you know," replied Achilles, also pleased to catch up with him.

They had known each other for years. They were some of the pioneers of the new system of informed consent and they had helped to design the vital functions of GAIC. Their working relationship had always been characterised by reciprocal respect, trust, and affection.

"Troubles... there are troubles," said the director-general. He had just spoken with an executive of the International Alliance for Agricultural Heritage.

"And?"

"And they are shocked beyond belief."

"I can imagine," was Achilles' only comment.

"There is a rumour that along with those seeds some other secret material was stored."

"Indeed."

"I don't know what was really stored in the vault. Unfortunately, the classified documents and protocols relating to the vault of Svalbard have disappeared from the archives of the International Alliance for Agricultural

Heritage. I have examined our records but could find not a single copy of these documents and protocols either, strange eh."

"When did they disappear from their archive?"

"A water damage was reported some six months ago and repairs were undertaken to fix it. These two events have been documented."

"I see…"

"Then two weeks ago an internal audit at the International Alliance revealed that an entire filing cabinet was missing. Unfortunately, it also contained the devices on which the files relating to the vault were saved. For some reasons, the files were classified since they contained data about the internal structure of the vault. The firm that carried out the repairs has denied any wrongdoing since nothing was removed by their workers from the archive."

"It sounds strange to me that the internal structure of the vault was viewed as classified information," Achilles said.

The director-general looked at him but made no comment. "We'll give you all the resources you need, without any restrictions," he declared, "try to solve the problem before the winter begins because there won't be many opportunities to go to the vault afterwards. Move fast, Achilles, very fast. Figure out what happened quickly."

"Informed consent requires time."

"This time, Achilles, we might not have much time." The director-general stood up and Achilles noticed that he was walking slowly, as if fatigued.

"This might be my last job, Achilles."

"See you later!"

The conversation left Achilles deeply worried. The director-general had delegated the whole matter to him. In thinking about the Svalbard vault, Achilles realised that he had not the slightest idea about what was at stake or who he was dealing with. His friend Claire Carlie in London came to mind. She was a geographer and an ecological historian. He decided to send her a message. Their different fields of knowledge and approaches often helped them to see problems from new angles.

"Do you have any interesting news about anything interesting?" Achilles wrote hastily. He knew that Claire would understand and carry out some research about hot spots and difficult issues before getting back to him. "Love to John and the kids."

He thought of lying down for a few minutes when a message from Bjarne appeared on the screen of his private device, to which only his family and friends had access.

"I am about to come up with some food and three people who want to see you."

Soon after a knock on the door was heard. It did not take Achilles long to understand that the people accompanying Bjarne were from the Norwegian government. Bjarne had brought a plate full of dry fruits, salmon and cheese, and some fresh bread baked by his partner, the hotel chef. After Bjarne had quit the room, Achilles turned to his visitors. The most distinguished of the three introduced himself as Colonel Dag Olsen, who was already known to Achilles through the leaked report. Olsen then made a formal introduction of the two people accompanying him, a representative of the Norwegian secret service and a member of the police.

"We have a difficult situation," said the colonel.

"Which situation are you speaking about?" replied Achilles.

"The vault of Svalbard has been vandalised and probably robbed!"

"I know."

"How come?" The colonel could barely hide his surprise.

"It seems," said Achilles in a slightly annoyed tone, "that some people wanted to inform us about the theft of the seeds and accordingly they've leaked a copy of 'your' classified report to me."

An embarrassed colonel looked at Achilles but said nothing, he regained his composure quickly, though, and apologised to Achilles. "Let no misgivings come between us."

Achilles shook the colonel's stretched hand and signalled that he was ready to move on.

The colonel gave more details away. "We think that the crime was committed one or two months ago. We will hopefully find out more during our upcoming expedition to the vault."

"I would like to be part of that expedition."

"It will be a military expedition," replied the colonel.

"Norway is the owner of the external vault, Colonel Olsen," Achilles said, "but considering the global emergency we are facing in Svalbard, ONO is now the legal owner of what is in the vault, no matter what it is."

"The polar bears belong to Norway," said the representative of the secret service.

"The polar bears belong to themselves," Achilles replied, "and as long as they are in the vault, they are under ONO's jurisdiction, like everything else that is in the vault."

The exchange reminded Norway's government of its place in the global chain of commands. In the end, it had mismanaged the security of the vault. After some considerations, Achilles and his visitors agreed that Norway and the military were to lead the mission to the vault but once the teams involved in the mission entered the building, Achilles or his nominated representatives would take over the command of the mission. As important as this clarification had been, it had certainly not been Achilles' intention to insist on a separation of competencies. He was well aware that no civilian, let alone ONO's top negotiator, would know how to fight a polar bear or armed robbers. They needed each other and they knew this but it was essential to remind each other of their roles and responsibilities.

"Who is going to accompany you?" Olsen asked without any sign of asperity in his voice. He knew Achilles' reputation far too well to even try to challenge him.

"Once I've selected my experts, I will pass on their names but you should roughly expect three more people." Achilles' answer was civil.

"And how many more will be working from the ONO headquarter?"

"Can't say for sure," Achilles replied, "but certainly twenty or more people."

"We need to move with caution," the colonel added in a tense voice.

"What else have you not told us?" Achilles asked the colonel, catching him by surprise. Olsen looked at him wondering if he could read thoughts.

"The documentation about the building and the storage rooms has disappeared."

"In other words?"

"In other words," Olsen replied, "we know little about the original firm that was involved in the construction of the vault. The Norwegian construction firm Byggesterk, which was contracted to build the vault, used subcontractors to carry out the job. Those subcontractors do not exist anymore. This means that we actually have no clue about what the whole internal structure of the vault looks like beyond the storage rooms."

"What do you know about the stored content?"

"To answer this question, an official permission is first needed," interjected the secret service official.

"In this case," Achilles said, "call the prime minister and ask her."

Calls were made. The chain of command was long in Norway but eventually they were able to reach the prime minister. Expectations, though, were going to be disappointed.

"We don't know what is stored in the vault except for the seeds," the prime minister declared visibly annoyed, "we bloody don't know if something else was stored," she added in an exasperated voice, "somebody has messed up or is messing up with us." Her aides looked nervous. The prime minister also said that the Norwegian government was trying to locate the whereabouts of the person who had been in charge of carrying out the first collection and storage of the world's seeds for the Nordic Alliance. All they knew was his name, Cary Flower. They were hoping that Flower would be able to shed some light on the events immediately preceding the opening of the vault and following the actual storage of the seeds. There was not much she could do for now. On that note, the prime minister left but not before apologising to Achilles for having to cancel their appointment scheduled for the afternoon to attend an urgent cabinet meeting.

This exchange also put an end to the visit. As he was rising from his chair, Olsen informed Achilles that the mission to the vault would take place in two days and depart from Oslo at dawn. "By then," he added, "we may know a bit more about everything and hopefully find the vault's architectural plan." The exact meeting point and time would be communicated to Achilles as soon as possible. He added that the mission would involve several soldiers, Achilles, his three experts, and finally two scientists, one nominated by the Norwegian government and one by the Nordic Alliance. If ONO so wished, the colonel added, it could nominate a scientist as well.

Achilles needed a break. He went down to the hotel bar in the hope that a change of scene, no matter how brief, would generate some new ideas.

"What happened?" Bjarne asked, looking worried.

"Something very bad," Achilles answered unable to say more, bound as he was by secrecy.

"Do me a favour, Bjarne," Achilles said with a serious look, "keep me informed about anyone who might come to your hotel and behave suspiciously or strangely."

Bjarne promised that he would. Achilles then had some lunch. If only he had more time and some more peace of mind to enjoy the delicious food prepared by the chef. An hour later, he returned to his room and decided to take a short break from all devices. He stretched out on his bed. *Think! I have to think hard!* He was a negotiator, always dealing with people but this time he was asked to look into a problem without knowing all of the parties involved. A negotiator like him brought people together and teased out problems. In this case, however, it seemed as if the situation in the Svalbard vault had turned things upside down by bringing problems together and separating people.

Chapter 4

Achilles was considering his next steps when he noticed that Angelo had sent him Åke Mio's private access code. He suddenly realised that Angelo was working late, hence in his reply he thanked him for his hard work and ordered him to go home to rest. Before signing off, Angelo told Achilles that he was missed by everyone, which made him smile. Achilles wasted no time and instantly sent a note to Mio asking for an urgent meeting. Expecting no immediate response from him and considering that Claire had not replied to his message yet, Achilles decided to go out for a walk. He was about to leave his room when a sound signalled the delivery of a message to his mailbox. It was from Mio.

"OK for a chat! Will call in five minutes!" Åke added that it was quite unusual to be contacted by ONO's top negotiator, "even for a professor of unsuality".

These Latinists, Achilles thought, *they know how to charm.*

He grabbed his device to make some notes and write down some questions but then he puzzled over how to best approach a professor of unsuality. And what is unsuality anyhow, he asked himself as if struck by a sudden intuition. He paused to reflect on the things that were happening.

Why the vault? Why Norway? This had been a quiet country for decades. There were no external enemies, conflicts were all internal, and when crime struck it hit the citizenry. He also thought that Norway was far too removed from the usual world's hot spots to be an unsafe country. Ha, perhaps this is why the theft seemed so unusual? But why the seeds? Certainly, if the climate continues to be as unpredictable as it had been of late food might become scarce. But are not our scientists already creating laboratory food? Would they be able to create enough to avert possible famines, should natural events turn unmanageable? What is unusual in all of this? This train of thought was stopped by a soft sound. Professor Mio was on the screen and the first thing he said to Achilles was to drop formalities. Achilles smiled at this typical Swedish attitude and from now on the professor was simply Åke.

"I know what happened!" exclaimed Åke.

"Hm, I won't enquire about your sources just now," Achilles replied. Then turning to the one issue that was on his mind, he asked Åke for his opinion.

"Why the vault?"

"Not sure," Åke replied, "it certainly looks a bit unusual to break into a fridge and steal seeds, unless there is a plan to run down food supplies." He paused as if critically evaluating the words he had just uttered. "But it does seem unlikely," he continued, "I mean, it could take a century before all food is gone, not to mention that the earth would have to be inundated in order for food to disappear completely, which could take another century. I mean, if you want to impress the world right now don't go to Svalbard, go to China and dissolve the Communist Party."

Slightly impatient, Achilles tried to steer the conversation in one direction by provoking Åke. "You seem to be as clueless as I am."

"What is your theory?"

"Have none so far. Yours?"

"Three issues seem unusual," Åke replied.

"The place, the act, and the bounty; if somebody wants to hold ONO to ransom by stealing its seeds…"

"The world's seeds," Achilles corrected him.

"Are there not two other collections?"

"There were two other collections of seeds," Achilles said, "one in Morocco, which has recently been destroyed during clashes between political factions, and one in San Francisco, which was burned down by the fire that followed the recent earthquake. And anyway, I've been informed that those two seed banks had stored only basic seeds such as rice, corn, potatoes, and tomatoes."

"On the other hand," resumed Åke, "why would anyone go to Svalbard and blow up the main door, kill some polar bears and steal the world's seeds?"

"Exactly!" interjected Achilles. "Why seeds and not atomic bombs or other weapons?"

"Because those things have been stolen already," was Åke's cool reply. And then as if an idea had just occurred to him, he slapped his forehead.

"Of course, that could be a reason."

"What?"

"Famine kills slowly," said Åke, "and it kills children first, then the poor, then the old, and so forth. As a tool of terror, famines are more effective than a bomb that kills many indiscriminately at the same time."

"So, famine is the new horror?" Achilles asked clearly terrified by the prospect of famines becoming the next weapons of mass destruction. He then realised that asking questions was the method used by negotiators when they work through cases and compare them before drawing conclusions. It was not Åke's method, though. Angelo, who knew Åke's teaching, had warned him that unusuality could not be approached through logical questions similarly to how scholasticism did in the past, because unusuality focuses on the counterintuitive, the unfamiliar, and the seemingly impossible to explain facts. To Achilles, this seemed a difficult approach, particularly because many of the certainties of the past had disappeared making it more difficult for people to relate to familiar things. Achilles was observing Åke attentively, catching every single movement of his body, hands, eyes, the small wrinkles forming around his mouth as he was speaking, the tense muscles of his face, the tone of his voice, the changing light in his eyes, the energy speeding through the veins of his hand. Attention to details was his strength, unsurpassed even by the notorious Japanese skill to master details. Achilles kept his eyes fixed on Åke's face as if trying to understand Åke's personality. Sensing Achilles' mounting doubts, Åke instantly said that in order to be able to help him, he would need to reconstruct what happened in the vault. Only by doing so, would he be able to extrapolate the unusual from the script. In other words, he had to go to the vault and see for himself.

"There is a mission going to Svalbard in two days," Achilles observed.

"That would do the trick," Åke declared. "I'll be in Oslo tomorrow night."

"OK. Join me where I am now," Achilles remarked without mentioning his whereabouts in Oslo, to which Åke replied with a smile.

After the conversation, Achilles decided to send some instructions to Angelo. He told Angelo that he wanted to assign some tasks to the three junior secretaries and was asking him to set a short morning meeting with them. He then asked Angelo to plan a two-hour meeting with all his senior aides. Achilles also urged Angelo to get the director-general to approve the immediate transfer of two scientific investigators, Martha and Roman, to Longyearbyen where he would meet them at the Svalbard Hotel on mission day.

Having done all he could to move ahead with the case, he decided to read anew the report leaked to him to check if he had not perhaps overlooked some important details. He was intent on studying the report when the assistant to the Norwegian interior minister was suddenly on the screen of his device. He confirmed that the mission to Svalbard was to take place in two days' time and take off from Oslo's old Fornebu airport at four in the morning. Achilles informed the assistant minister that professor Åke Mio was going to be in his team. The assistant took note but made no comment. Achilles also mentioned the names of the two ONO investigators who were to assist him for the duration of the investigation. Again, the assistant wrote down the information imparted to him but made no comment.

"Please inform the minister and let me know if there are any problems with my team." In the spirit of cooperation, Achilles wanted to include the Norwegian interior minister in his choice of experts.

It was nearly five in the afternoon when Achilles decided to go out and enjoy Oslo's fresh air. He walked from the hotel down to Karl Johan's Gate and admired the beautiful tree-lined avenue leading up to the royal palace. He continued walking toward the central station where one of Oslo's most intriguing symbols was publicly displayed. A gigantic bronze sculpture of a crawling tiger; solitary and proud, it seemed to remind humans of the ever-presence of animals. He was very fond of it. He kept walking until he perceived the salty smell of the sea and the crisp breeze coming up from the city fiord. He looked up and noticed the Milky Way. He wondered how many more still unknown ways were up there in the wide space. *But are they actually leading somewhere?*

When he returned to the hotel, Achilles went to the restaurant and admired the buffet prepared for the guests. Norway knew how to treat its visitors. Again, he was annoyed at his having so little time to enjoy such a feast. He gave himself an hour to appreciate the food prepared by his host. He deeply felt the importance of food and realised for the first time since the Svalbard crisis, what a food shortage could mean to people.

Chapter 5

When Achilles returned to his room, he went quickly through the notes he had prepared for the two-video meeting he was going to chair on the following day. As he was just about to add some final entries to his memos, a request for access flashed on the screen of his private device. It was Claire.

"What are you up to?" Achilles was eager to know how his friend had spent her time since their last conversation.

"I've been to Alice Springs in Central Australia and have just returned from a trip to the desert," replied Claire.

"Hm. Why the desert?"

"I'm following up some new research suggesting that deserts are changing."

"Meaning?"

"The *New National Geographic* recently published a story about some areas in the northern African desert which are said to be slowly retreating. Similar ideas were advanced some years ago by two academic journals, *Biogeosciences* and the *New Scientist*, and lately several researchers at the University of Amsterdam and the University of Copenhagen have also observed a retreat of the desert in west-African countries along the belt that stretches from Burkina Faso up to the Red Sea. More recently, scientists at the Max Institute for

Meteorology in Berlin have shown that the air in those regions has a new water-holding capacity that can facilitate the regeneration of plants and stabilisation of the soil. New vegetation is growing, agricultural land is expanding."

"And you went to Central Australia to see if the desert is changing there too?"

"Exactly. I met with researchers and scientists from the local university and went to the desert with them and several Aboriginal rangers. But it was a bit difficult, at least for me, to notice any sign of sand retreat, perhaps due to the fact that Australian deserts are moderately arid and semi-arid, meaning that the influence of climate there is more general than specific."

"Does this mean that a possible change of climate might have less impact on that part of the Australian desert?"

"Possibly," she answered, "but I would need to research the matter further."

"But what do the Aborigines say?"

"The opinions are split," Claire added that for some Aboriginal communities the desert was important for dream or myth interpretation. She also mentioned that after the discovery of a grotto with ancient wall drawings many Aborigines believed that there were ruins of past settlements buried under the sand and looked positively to the desert shrinking. They continued talking about the implications of such developments till a change of topic put Achilles on the spot.

"And what have you been up to?" she then asked.

Achilles did not reply immediately. He wondered if he was bound by secrecy toward scientists such as Claire. She sensed his hesitation and, guessing that he might be dealing with classified issues, suggested that he just tell her what was not classified and that she would piece the story together herself.

"I'm in Oslo and the day after tomorrow, I'm going on an official mission to Longyearbyen in the Svalbard archipelago."

Claire immediately saw the Nordic landscape before her. She figured out that there could be only two reasons for Achilles to go to Svalbard. Either there was a meeting on climate change or there was a meeting on the seed vault. If there had been a meeting on climate, Claire inferred, she would certainly have been informed about it or even invited to it but as this was not the case, she concluded that Achilles was going to the vault.

"Has something happened to the vault?"

Achilles admired her perspicacity.

"Robbed."

"What? You're kidding me."

"Nope."

"Of all the seeds?"

"Not sure. Will have to see for myself what happened."

"I can't believe it!" Claire's expression made Achilles realise even more strongly the tragic importance of the theft. He recalled his conversation with Åke about food shortages.

"Do you think that somebody could try to artificially induce global famines?"

"Heaven!" Claire cried horrified by the idea. She had witnessed food shortages in some of the areas where she had carried out research as a PhD student in geographic history. She quickly recovered, however, and soon was able to think analytically.

"To create a global famine crisis, food would have to disappear completely from a vast region, and at the same time, the availability of food in some other, less affected regions would also have to reduce for some reasons... but why would something like that happen?"

"Because of diminished food productions caused by a farming crisis?" asked Achilles.

"But it would take quite a long while for such a crisis to have a global impact. There exist big reserves of corn, wheat, rice, potatoes, and tomatoes, as far as I know, not to count many reserves of fruits."

"Ah, that's good," replied Achilles with some relief in his voice, "where are the reserves?"

"Not sure," replied Claire, "isn't Organisation Number One in charge of food reserves?"

"I'd think so," said Achilles. A pause followed which was broken by his asking her under what circumstances a global famine could occur.

"Only if a total lack of food were to happen in many places and at the same time."

"Hm." Achilles seemed absentminded but she would not press him for more information.

"When are you going to inform the world about the Svalbard theft?"

"After my visit to the vault."

"Anyone special coming with you?"

"Åke Mio," replied Achilles.

"Ha!" was Claire's comment.

"Do you know him?"

"Only as a scientist, not personally. He's a smart guy." She continued explaining that the year before, Mio had attended a climate change conference in Iceland which attracted the best and brightest in the field. Claire said that Mio was one of the keynote speakers and that, as always with him, a big crowd came to his talk.

"What is his position on climate?" Achilles asked.

"Mio never takes a position on any issue," replied Claire, catching Achilles by surprise, "he's interested in things that scientists cannot follow up, the unusual and that kind of thing."

"Why, aren't you scientists doing the same?"

"Oh, no," replied Claire, "scientists focus on norms and the deviations from the norms and draw conclusions. The more data they have to support one or the other, the happier they are." After a brief pause, she added that today's science, particularly geography, was based on data-driven models. "We don't look at the sky and moon to figure out whether the following day will bring rain or sun."

"That's a pity, no?" replied Achilles. This time it was Claire to be caught by surprise by her friend's remark.

"When Mio gave his speech at the Iceland conference," continued Claire, "he criticised the scientists. He said: 'If you can reproduce the climate through your modelling, as you claim, then climate is perhaps not the big phenomenon that you say it is, then how can a force that can supposedly destroy the earth be caught in a model?'"

"Interesting," Achilles said.

"Some colleagues," Claire continued, "asked him if he had not perhaps overlooked the floods and fires, the recurring and expanding droughts, and the disappearance of plants and animals."

"And what did he reply?"

"Mio never replies to provocative questions," was Claire answer.

Achilles checked the time, he felt exhausted and in serious need of rest. He mentioned this to Claire and suggested they get in touch after his mission to the vault.

"Can I tell John?" she asked.

"Yes," Achilles answered, "but it can't go any further than John just now."

Chapter 6

On the following day, at two in the afternoon in Oslo, Achilles was ready to dock into his office station to chair the two meetings he had asked Angelo to organise for him. It was just eight in the morning in New York; the vault emergency had made everybody adjust to Achilles' European time. Before accepting his position as second in charge after the director-general, Achilles had outlined a number of clear conditions. He had requested and been granted, a budget that would allow him to create an office space that was conducive to a productive and peaceful atmosphere. He was also able to hire several senior assistants to whom he could delegate tasks during his frequent visits to the ONO members, the money also allowed him to give all his staff the opportunity to improve their skills through professional development. It was Achilles' rule that no decisions should be based on theoretical modelling or forecasts alone; he wanted to travel and see things for himself, meet with people, tease out the various interests involved in negotiations. When he could not travel in person, one of his senior assistants would go instead and collect as many facts as possible about all the issues at stake.

Achilles' office had 120 permanent staff members, and this number included himself and his personal assistant

Angelo, ten senior and ten junior scientific aides, the head negotiator and his ten senior and ten junior assistant negotiators, the head rhetorician and her ten senior and ten junior assistants, three junior secretaries and four interns. In addition, there were ten expert representing various scientific disciplines, two trusted external scientists, ten IT experts and technology developers, ten programmers, ten scientists from the humanities, the chef and three of his crew in the café-bar and kitchen, and finally the three members of the cleaning crew. The role of the interns was part of Achilles' succession plan for GAIC, which he introduced immediately after joining the ONO. Achilles had anticipated that internships would last two years for every cohort of interns and that at the end of the training, those who had proven themselves capable of working within the agency were offered a junior position. The current interns had just arrived. They were Ajana from Africa, Emily from the United States, Fatin from the Middle East and Luca from Europe. Interns carried out work for Angelo or for the junior secretaries but were also mentored by the senior members of the office.

The GAIC office included big and small rooms, mezzanines, and some working spaces suspended between the various floors. The whole space, some 8,000 square inches, was filled with light, and every room including the bathrooms, had functional windows. To be able to open the windows and enjoy fresh air was a real privilege. Paintings and sculptures from artists were sources of creativity and inspiration to all staff. The kitchen was big and luminous, as were the café and restaurant, managed by a chef who delighted everybody with his weekly creations and by letting the members of staff vote for the best monthly dish. These activities helped everyone relax and never lose sight of the simple things in life. Everyone was responsible for the tasks assigned to them and when difficulties arose between parties or between working units, they were resolved consensually. Expectations were high but so too were solidarity and collaboration and when overtime was required, those involved could take time off once the assigned projects were completed.

GAIC was undoubtedly a unique place; one could travel through the world and never find anything comparable to it. It was also the most vibrant agency within ONO, and the most powerful too. Everybody who worked there made an effort to spend time together leisurely, something that often happened during lunch. And who would ever miss the delicious food prepared by chef Romeo? He and Achilles had known each other for a long time. Romeo had worked in the London residence of his uncle and when Achilles accepted the director position at GAIC, he brought Romeo with him. Romeo was also Achilles' confidant, always in the know about the latest happenings as well as the glamour and gossip that were part of the hospitality world; the celebrities of the moment, where they dined, how they lived, and so forth. But Romeo was more than that. He was also a biochemist, who knew that good food implied safe food, which is why he bought food only in selected stores. He prepared his food with the same care as the old pharmacists who mixed medical compounds; food for him was medicine for both body and mind. His reputation made him a sought-after judge at many cooking competitions, and a food consultant for all local schools that had introduced warm meals for their pupils.

The lunches at the GAIC were always a time for sharing niceties and new ideas or impressions of new books, sports activities, concerts, and so forth. The collegial atmosphere that reigned at GAIC helped everybody balance their work and life productively, while the single and young could bond with each other in a safe environment.

The three junior secretaries Achilles was briefing this morning were Annabelle, Lucillo and Parys. He had met them several years before, more precisely during the first informed consent negotiations over which he had presided. They had remained in contact ever since and once they had completed their studies; they wrote to him to apply for internships. He still remembered reading their letters with pleasure.

Annabelle had studied negotiation and literature at her local university. She had been accepted into a PhD program to study the language of negotiation. Her idea was to work as an intern while she was completing her doctoral thesis. Through an internship at GAIC, she wrote to him, she would get some direct access to the negotiators and gain some special insights into the workings of negotiations. Achilles admired her determination and approved her application instantly.

Lucillo had studied philosophy at his local university. Afterwards, he had applied for a PhD place to study negotiation and rhetoric, and the university had accepted his candidature. Later, he would decide whether he wanted to become a negotiator or join the rhetoricians. An internship at GAIC, he wrote in his application, would give him the opportunity to watch negotiators and rhetoricians at work while completing his doctorate thesis. As always with Lucillo, caution and consideration were important. Achilles approved his application without hesitation.

Parys had studied physical engineering and genetics at a technology institute. He had also volunteered as a nurse at Hospital General in Boston. At these two places, he met some of the most skilled engineers in nanotechnology and neuroscience. One of these was his professor in motoric and robotic. When Achilles met young Parys, the boy used to move around on a scooter due to an illness that had weakened his leg muscles. Recently, he had undergone a successful operation, carried out by his professor in collaboration with neuroscientists, which represented a breakthrough in neuro-motoric and engineering. As a result, Parys could walk again. He too had been offered a PhD place in robotics but although he had accepted it, he had also asked permission to postpone the starting date of his research. He told his professors that he wanted to enjoy his walking body. His wish was granted and now he supported a charity that helped people with motoric difficulties. His ambition was to help shape policies that could benefit those who like him had to master body issues in addition to their youth. GAIC, he told Achilles, would be the right place for exploring policies promoting positive diversity. Achilles loved Parys' letter which was full of joy and plans for himself and others, and he approved his internship immediately.

During today's meeting, Achilles explained the tasks he wanted the three junior secretaries to carry out. He asked Lucillo to find out if NASA or any other national space agency had planned settlements on Mars or the Moon, and if this involved the establishment of food banks. Annabelle was to study how climate scientists modelled droughts and flooding across the world, including the modelling of problems in small communities or sparsely populated areas.

And he wanted Parys to try to find collectors of rare plants and endangered seeds and find out how they stored them, the types of storehouses they used, and if possible, how they protected the collections. Achilles had set aside a travel budget for them, which they could use freely to visit people or sites that were important for the execution of their assignments. The four interns, Achilles said, would support them in all their efforts. Finally, he let them know that his senior assistants had been asked to mentor and help them when needed. As always, Achilles reminded them about time management and the need to stay focused on their tasks.

Achilles had asked Angelo to schedule a second meeting with his senior assistants and GAIC scientists. The director-general had also expressed a desire to attend the meeting, which proved that ONO considered the theft of the seeds to be a global emergency. After some initial greetings and small talk, Achilles asked whether any famine crises had recently been reported to the ONO agencies. One of his senior staff, George Lee, replied that indeed two reports had been filed to the urgent attention of the food department and that he was examining them for GAIC. Achilles then asked if the architectural plan of the Svalbard vault had been located.

"Yes, it has been retrieved," replied Martha White, a marine biologist and ocean physicist. "Adam and I managed to crack a classified program that protected the plan which was, in turn, saved on an old device belonging to the defunct NU."

Martha was one of the two scientists who was going to accompany Achilles to the upcoming mission to the Svalbard vault. She was to meet him on the following day in the Svalbard Hotel. Adam Featherstone was another expert in

Achilles' team, a technological genius who could solve almost any kind of problems.

"The architectural plan was buried under a pile of data," Martha added.

The task of explaining the plan fell upon Roman Lutowski. Adam and Martha had asked him for assistance in interpreting the plan since he was a civil engineer and an expert in materials. Roman was also going to join the team going the vault the next day. After examining the architectural plan Roman declared that there was a three-thousand feet long way on it – a tight tunnel piercing the mountain. The tunnel ended in front of four doors leading to the storage hall.

"Judging from the type of construction," Roman said, "the temperature in the corridor might be about 5 Fahrenheit." Roman also pointed out that the doors had no door handles. Instead, door one, two and four had a square placed on their left-hand side, which he understood to be a device that functioned as an electronic key. "The odd thing is that on the third door, the same square is placed on the right-hand side!" Roman concluded his explanation by saying that the vault's main entrance had no lock or handle.

"This points to an algorithm as the opening key," interjected Adam.

"The firm that looked after the security of the vault, and certainly the scientists who went into it must have the access code, no?" George asked.

"I've been told by the representatives of the Nordic Alliance that once all of the seeds were classified, the scientists looking after them went to the vault only every six months to check the temperature and the status of the seeds and that on these occasions they were accompanied by the security people," replied Achilles.

"Can we talk to them?"

"Colonel Olsen wanted to pay a visit to the security firm. Let's see what he has to say tomorrow."

"Because the main entrance was blown apart," Martha interjected at this point, "does this mean that the thieves did not know the algorithm?"

"Possibly," said Adam, "but still they must have had the algorithms to the storage doors."

"I wonder what might be the link between the ropes and the main entrance been blown apart?" Here no one had an answer to Achilles' question and it seemed too audacious at this early stage of the investigation to speculate about such a possible link.

While they were having this discussion, Achilles received a video call from Olsen. Achilles instantly informed the colonel that he was presently in a meeting with some of his senior staff who would be able to listen to his communication. Olsen did not seem to mind. He had in fact greater worries than this, something that became apparent when he started to speak.

"Unfortunately, the government has not been able to find the original copy of the internal plan of the vault. So yesterday, I decided to pay a visit to Byggesterk, the construction firm that built the vault, to see if they had it. It turned out that they had no copy on their files either, which was very disappointing. They, however, showed me a copy of a hand-drawn plan of the vault, which was all they had. I took a closer look at the plan, with the help of the military civil engineers accompanying me, but we could neither ascertain with absolute certainty how many storage rooms there were on the plan nor how many doors there were in the storage hall. Sounds strange, I know."

"Did you mention this to Byggesterk?" Achilles asked.

"I certainly did, and they too were a bit surprised at first, till somebody suggested that the handwritten plan could depict an enclosed space. When I asked for clarification, one of their architects or engineers replied that the drawing seemed to depict a section of the vault which was presumably the storage area."

"Only a partial plan?" Achilles asked disappointed.

"It seems!"

Achilles did not know what to say but he urged the colonel to employ all his resources to find the original plan of the vault before tomorrow's mission. Olsen understood that there must be a reason why Achilles was urging him to find the plan, and in taking the hint, the colonel ended the conversation but not before reminding Achilles that he was going to collect him and his guest the next day at dawn.

The meeting continued with Achilles wondering why the doors had not been clearly marked out on the drawing. In the meantime, Martha had projected on a large office screen the plan she and Adam had retrieved the day before. Everybody saw the tunnel end in front of four doors, which everybody considered to be the doors opening into the storage hall. At this point, Adam stood up and smilingly said that he would now show them some algorithmic magic.

"A few weeks ago," he continued, "an IT firm from Silicon Valley asked me to review a program for the US Defence Department which the firm had developed in collaboration with the Massachusetts Institute of A.I. The program is secret, totally classified, under intellectual property laws. It is quite a complex type of program, I must say. For this reason, Defence required it to be reviewed by external experts with no conflicts of interest. These experts had to include the best independent programmers currently on the market. I was not included in the list of the reviewers because I work for ONO. So the IT firm asked the reviewers selected by Defence to test the program. Interestingly, none of them could really deliver, because to test such a complex program one really needs something that is just as complex, which no one seemed to have. In other words, no one had an object against which the program could be tested. That was the first hurdle. The second one is, obviously, that the reviewers must be smarter than the program itself in order to understand the program's virtues and deficiencies. It appears that none of the people could satisfy these two conditions. So, the firm and Defence turned to me."

Adam made this statement in total humility but Achilles and the others perfectly understood that if they had called on Adam, it was probably because he was the best, and it also meant that Defence and the American government still trusted Adam, even though he was now with ONO. Adam had been an academic programmer and IT engineer for many years; he himself had developed computer programs and invented some of the successful devices that were now in use. Before quitting his research job he had also created some remarkable A.I. applications. One day, almost out of the blue, he felt that he needed more meaning in his life, that he wanted to do work in ways that helped people to live better. He wrote to Achilles, whom he admired, and asked to work with him. From the first day in Achilles' office, Adam showed not only his skills but also his caring style by always being prepared to help and listen. It was obvious to everybody that his level of mathematical knowledge was very high and that no one at ONO could match his computational abilities but he did not mind. He had never felt more emotionally balanced than he was now at GAIC. He still had plenty of friends and colleagues at his previous workplace, whom he helped when they asked for assistance, and whom he turned to when he needed some help.

"So," Adam continued, "I agreed to review the program, after obtaining permission from Achilles, and at first I thought that it would be business as usual. But soon I had to admit that the program to be tested was quite sophisticated, of a kind I had never dealt with before. And if I had such difficulties, I concluded, Defence must have had even more. But given the complexity of the program, I now wonder if the developers themselves are still in control of their creation," Adam paused and then turned to Achilles.

"Which is why, faced with such difficulties, I recently asked you to extend your permission to continue the review over a longer period of time."

"I remember," replied Achilles.

"So," continued Adam, "just by going through some segments of the program, I understood that to test it, I would need an extraordinary object, which indeed I didn't have until after Martha and I found the abandoned architectural plan of the Svalbard vault."

When Adam said this, everybody was startled at first but by now they knew him well enough to know that something very special was going to follow.

"After discussing the plan of the vault with Martha and Roman," Adam went on, "I decided to run the Defence's program on it, and here is what I saw."

Adam replaced the plan of the Svalbard vault that Martha had projected on the big office screen with the same plan, but this time read through the program he was reviewing for Defence. He then asked them to identify how many doors were on the plan. Everybody saw four doors. In no time, he pressed some keys, ran through some data, calculated some parameters, and finally, some very fine, almost imperceptible red lines appeared along the second and the third doors. No lines were visible along the first and fourth doors.

"How ingenious!" Roman exclaimed.

As the others were looking confused, Adam added some colours to the spaces separated by the lines. "Imagine standing in front of the doors," he said. They all looked at the doors on the screen and suddenly saw, with the help of the measurements projected by Adam onto the screen, that all of the doors were 80 inches wide and 80 inches high. As Adam continued his calculations, other dotted lines, this time yellow, appeared on the screen. They highlighted a small door panel contained in door two which was 20 inches wide, and an equally sized small panel contained in door three. Put together those inches built a small door which was 40 inches wide and set between doors two and three. This meant that, practically, only three-quarters of the second and third doors opened.

"The reason why the electronic square on the third door is placed on the right-hand side," said Adam at this point turned to Roman, "is because that door opens from right to left, while doors one, two and four, open from left to right." People using the second or third door, Adam added, would not easily realise that one-third of their panels remained inaccessible. "And even if somebody were to notice this, its significance would be overlooked."

"Five doors!" exclaimed Achilles. He looked at the director-general in total disbelief.

After a short silence marked by tension the director-general spoke, "Remember," said he, "that we have inherited this responsibility, and that all NU people who were involved in the project of the Svalbard vault have left by now."

"Are the doors protected by a mathematical formula?" Achilles asked.

"I believe so," was Adam's prompt reply, "but I don't know how yet. I'll have to keep testing the program I am reviewing to find out."

"So, the program you had to test, whatever it is and whatever it is intended for," Achilles said, "seems to work."

"It does," said Adam, "but there are still some issues I'd like to discuss with some professors at Mountain View and in Massachusetts, where I previously taught, if you don't mind," said Adam turned to Achilles.

"Go ahead, Adam, they'll be thrilled to hear your latest stories."

"Hey, but doesn't this mean that somebody is ahead of us and has a far more advanced program to protect the doors than any of us?" asked Martha.

"Sorry if I earlier expressed myself incorrectly," replied Adam, "only the hidden door is protected by what I am inclined to call an advanced algorithm. A simple algorithm might be enough to open the other doors, which is why the thieves, perhaps mathematicians or IT experts, succeeded in cracking it so easily. And to reply to your questions, yes, I think that some people are far ahead of us and Defence."

Visibly shaken by the way the events were developing, the director-general promised to give more resources to GAIC to help get the case solved as soon as possible. "Come on guys, be quick. Be quicker!" Hereafter, he thanked everybody and left the room.

The discussion now turned to other issues, such as the importance of the world's seeds and the danger of artificially induced food crises. Before winding down the meeting, Achilles reminded his aides of the upcoming mission to the vault scheduled for the following day, Thursday. He also informed them that the ONO director-general was planning to send out a global communiqué about the theft of the seeds on the coming Friday. The meeting did not continue for much longer, and soon Achilles switched off the remote channel. It was now late afternoon in Oslo and Achilles felt like he needed a break. He went for a walk.

Chapter 7

The November air was fresh, the sky clear. Achilles felt strangely nostalgic and longing for distant places where no problems were awaiting him. He reached the pier. The sea was calm and unaware of all the troubles that humans were causing to themselves. It had been an exciting and intense period the last five years at ONO, particularly within GAIC. He had helped to implement the system of informed consent in all the member states. Certainly, there were still a few problems to sort, particularly in the regions prone to slide back into past systems of coercion and tribunals regulated by old laws. Achilles had worked hard to contain opposition to GAIC and its system of negotiation. The traditional law profession at first resisted the introduction of the new system but when the advantage of reaching informed consent through negotiation became apparent, opposition quickly disappeared.

Achilles had not created the doctrine of informed consent but he had been one of the first negotiators to apply it successfully. He had also been influential in improving the instruments of informed consent after its introduction as the foundation of all legal systems. Informed consent meant that all disputes between parties, no matter their nature, required a consensual solution and that such solution should be grounded in processes of informed decision making. To help informed consent become the guiding principle between parties in disputes, ONO had created the role of the rhetoricians. Their sole task was to help people reach informed consent in matters that dealt with divisive issues, and this actually meant that the resolution of disputes was not the task of the rhetoricians. Rhetoricians operated within the boundaries of negotiations set by GAIC, in cooperation with the negotiators. The agency, more precisely its top negotiator, had the power to call and host global negotiations in response to requests submitted by individuals, organisations, and groups of people. All negotiators, senior and junior, reported to Achilles and so did the rhetoricians.

Negotiators and rhetoricians worked side by side but because the role of the former consisted in scrutinising the work of the latter, negotiators had a clear advantage over rhetoricians. Such advantage consisted in having the power to set limits to rhetoric. This was not an easy task, though, considering that rhetoricians had logic and language skills that most negotiators did not possess.

Only a few decades earlier, lawyers had controlled all kinds of conflicts between people, between people and organisations, and organisations and institutions. Money was the currency that sustained the old laws. This is not to say that there were no principles but when the courts and judges were weak, those principles could be tweaked in whatever way one wanted. Informed consent, however, could not be tweaked because it implied an underlying objective understanding that the parties to a dispute had to share. When the NU collapsed and the patchy law that had regulated its workings became evident to the point of disgust, people and governments decided to create ONO. The name Organisation Number One was intended to highlight its importance in the global hierarchy of decision making. At that time, it was also decided that GAIC would become ONO's main agency. Five years ago, Achilles was invited to join GAIC and replace the outgoing director. On accepting the offer, he instantly also became the top negotiator of the ONO. By the time of his promotion Achilles had already presided over several major negotiations and won the admiration of people and professionals. As a top negotiator, Achilles helped countries and institutions to embrace informed consent by reinventing their social life and the norms that should regulate it.

The walk brought clarity to his mind and soon his thoughts turned to Adam. He dwelled on the program that Adam had been asked to test for Defence and wondered if, in the future, a successful response to new challenges was going to require an informed consent strengthened by artificial intelligence. Whether tomorrow's battles were to be fought with algorithms rather than conventional weapons? He took a deep breath. The cold November air travelled quickly through his nostrils and lungs. The oxygen revitalised his whole body. He recapitulated the recent events mentally, still feeling the impact of the information imparted by Adam about a hidden door protected by a program that probably only a few could crack. How is informed consent supposed to win against such new elites? This question made him impatient, almost restless.

Informed consent was a young doctrine. It was competing with old powers and governments that had opposed it from the beginning. Some of these governments were run by autocrats who despised GAIC and the notion of informed consent. Perhaps, the real target of the theft was not the vault of Svalbard but GAIC and informed consent. By sabotaging GAIC, some people might try to undermine ONO, as they had undermined NU in the past. But Achilles knew that ONO was different and one of its advantages was that politicians had been banned from it. Governments could name experts but they would not sit at a table with their political friends and make decisions about the world. That time had passed and no one wanted it back. To stay strong, however, ONO had to be the best, which means that it had to be ahead of governments and their national services. GAIC was still a young agency, if compared to traditional institutions, nonetheless, it had been able to remove many injustices, bestow new rights on children and fortify the status of many cities. Children were no longer stripped of basic rights; they could fight against poverty according to their needs, they could leave parents that neglected them and claim a right to speak, to have an education and healthcare. Cities like London had opposed decisions handed down by the central government to allow foreign powers to place agents in their suburbs, use municipalities to channel illegal money into dirty activities and buy whole city streets. Some cities became so successful in managing their freedom and resources that they now resembled new city-states and city republics. They had signed contracts of protection with ONO, although they were still able to continue cooperation with their governments and other national regions.

Big clouds had spread over the sky leaving only a luminous strip down on the horizon. Achilles turned his gaze towards it, only to discover that the light was so strong as to blind him. He looked at the city from the pier. *A sleeping tiger*, he thought. Checking the time, he noticed that two hours had passed.

Chapter 8

Achilles returned to the hotel and found Bjarne waiting for him. He informed him that Åke Mio had arrived and asked about him. Assuming that Åke would soon join him for dinner, Achilles decided to spend some time with his friend, and the two set down together enjoying the hot chocolate that Bjarne had prepared for Achilles. They spoke about sports, movies, exhibitions and all the themes that were dear to them. Bjarne avoided talking about work and Achilles was grateful for that because he would not have been able to answer any questions.

"Is there a Norwegian mentality?" Achilles asked with nonchalance while taking the first sip of his chocolate. "Hm," he then whispered, "it's delicious."

"I think there is," Bjarne said. "We Norwegians have built a close-knit society, we like the world from our perspective but we don't want the world to come to us, which is why we dislike tourism. Tourism is a plague and won't be easy for a small country like ours to stop it before we end up like Florence, Venice, London, Paris and New York which have all become restless places. For Norway, the danger also comes from the sea with all the environmental problems caused by big cruisers docking in our ports."

Achilles was listening attentively. Bjarne seemed to feel strongly about these issues and Achilles longed to know if he had missed to notice it in the past or if Bjarne's passions had changed. Bjarne had been a brilliant student but had never much patience for authority and often clashed with his professors. After the conclusion of his studies, he returned to Oslo where he spent a year trying to figure out what he wanted to do with a legal degree and no wish to pursue graduate studies. At first, he got involved in local politics and he was successful. Then he tried federal politics. Here too, he was at first successful but when he realised that he lacked the sangfroid that keeps politicians alive, and after acknowledging this to himself, he turned his back on public life. His parents owned a little hotel in an elegant part of Oslo, a boutique hotel with just forty rooms. Bjarne had always imagined that he would sell it as soon as his parents retired but his experiences in politics made him change his mind. When his parents left the business to him, some years later, he transformed it into one of Oslo's most elegant hotels. It became his world. There he would meet diplomats, journalists, scientists, rich artists and all kind of people who wanted a well-functioning place full of comforts. Achilles always got a suite there.

"Are there many people who think like you?" Achilles asked, breaking the pause that followed Bjarne's speech.

"Yes," answered Bjarne, "you see, if our politicians can't manage tourism, how can they be expected to know how to manage migration and refugees flows?"

"Aren't the two issues different?" asked Achilles.

"They are," Bjarne quickly replied, "which is why they require different policies but global politics has not differentiated between them at all, contributing to the destruction of national identities."

As important as these issues were, Achilles wished for small talk to preserve some serenity. In noticing Achilles' silence, Bjarne changed the topic of their conversation.

"How is your mother?"

"She's fine," Achilles replied relieved, "she now lives with Uncle William in England. I will drop by on my way back to New York."

While they were talking, Åke entered the room and greeted Achilles. He had an athletic posture, not the usual bent academic body. Achilles smiled back to his friendly eyes and good features. They talked about his flight and the weather and soon moved toward the restaurant but not before Achilles had thanked Bjarne for his chocolate extraordinaire and after putting his arm around Bjarne's shoulders, Achilles informed him that he was leaving on the following morning at four o'clock and returning on Friday evening. Bjarne promised him a good breakfast and then they shook hands affectionately. The dinner with Åke passed without any remarkable occurrence. Both tried to avoid speaking about the issue that had brought them together, intent on leaving it for the next day.

When Achilles went down to the breakfast room at daylight he found Bjarne already up and setting the table. He was soon joined by Åke who seemed to be in a good mood. Bjarne wished his friend and his guest a good trip. He was aware that Achilles was on a mission and he was impatient to hear more about it. He knew that Achilles would share all of the unclassified information with him and ask Bjarne for his impressions and opinions. Achilles was his dearest friend, and they always helped each other to deal with life matters.

"Remember your promise," Achilles said to Bjarne when Colonel Olsen appeared in the hall.

"I will keep my eyes and ears wide open," replied Bjarne.

Chapter 9

When they reached Olsen's vehicle, Achilles noticed that there were several people sitting in it. Introductions followed and some formalities were discussed. After reaching the airport, which happened quicker than Achilles had expected, they rapidly transferred to a plane and a few minutes later, they were breaking through a thick layer of clouds. They arrived at Longyearbyen airport at six. Olsen and the other officials went to the Longyearbyen military base while Achilles and Åke were accompanied by soldiers to the Svalbard Hotel, from where they were picked up an hour later. On entering the hotel, Achilles found Martha and Roman waiting for him. They greeted each other affectionately before everybody went quickly to their rooms to dress for the next trip to the island of Spitsbergen, the last human settlement before the Svalbard vault.

Martha and Roman had brought a suitcase for Achilles that contained winter clothes for the journey. Achilles had asked his neighbours Juanita and Carlos to pack his winter clothes and take them to his GAIC office. Juanita was a private dance teacher and Carlos was an electric engineer working for an international electricity company. To add to their income, Juanita had been looking after Achilles' place three days a week for the past two years. They had four children, Manolo who was seven, Senorita who was five, and the twins Pablo and Rosetta who were four. Six months ago, Juanita had asked Achilles for help in finding an affordable apartment. They had been evicted from their present place. The other tenants, said she, found their children too noisy. Achilles owned a townhouse that included two large units and a generous garden. He occupied one but the other had been standing empty for some time. The entrances to the two units were on the same level, too close for comfort, which is why Achilles never rented the place. When Juanita mentioned her situation, he instantly told her to come and stay in his house. As tempting as this offer was, Juanita realised that they would not be able to pay the rent since Achilles' house was located in one of New York's finest residential neighbourhoods and the apartment he was offering was a very large and elegant place, far beyond what they could afford. She also did not want to live there at his expenses, so much for her pride. She mentioned this to Achilles to which he spontaneously replied, "If so, just pay what you paid for the other place."

It did not take Juanita very long to overcome her hesitation. She was not one of those people who need lots of persuasion if something feels right; by now she had known Achilles far too well to suppose that he did not mean what he said. All things considered, she felt that she could honestly take the offer. She called a moving firm and the following day she and her family were living next to him. When Achilles returned home that night, he found four little drawings on his living room table and a wonderful dinner ready to eat. Juanita had kept his keys and would continue to look after his place as she had done before. In the end, nothing had changed in their arrangement except that he now had a lively family living next door.

When Achilles opened the suitcase, he found a drawing by Senorita. On the drawing, a family of polar bears, two adults and two offspring, were walking towards a shore. The smaller bear had his head turned toward a man standing five yards away and dressed in a dark suit, his blue eyes fixed on those of the little bear. Achilles took the drawing in his hands and admired Senorita's skills. He thought that just by drawing a few lines she had created a masterpiece. He put the drawing on the desk, dressed quickly and returned to the hall where the others were waiting for him.

When they met outside the hotel, Olsen informed Achilles that three helicopters were going to be involved in today's mission and that two had already left while the third was waiting for him and the civilian team. He also told Achilles that the government had finally succeeded in retrieving the original plan of the vault. Continuing his speech in the helicopter, Olsen added that he was also able to share information about the IT firm that had installed the original security system in the vault. The firm had been bought by some other firm immediately after the installation of the system and then sold many more times till approximately five years ago it had been acquired by the firm that was presently looking after the security system of the entire vault. In response, Achilles asked the colonel if he had had the time to check the plan of the vault, to which Olsen replied that he had, and so had the Norwegian government. He stated that there were four doors and that he expected them to be open.

"Who did the original security firm report to and who is the present one reporting to?" Achilles asked.

"To the Norwegian government on behalf of the Nordic Alliance and ONO," replied the colonel.

Achilles glanced at Martha and Roman sitting on his left. Olsen turned to Achilles with a surprised look. He had expected him to say something but his silence worried him.

"Is it not so?"

"If you say so," replied Achilles. He then added that he had no information about any accredited IT firm that had created, installed, and updated the security in the Svalbard vault. This piece of information troubled Colonel Olsen and the other Norwegians but no comments were made by any of them, leaving everybody unsatisfied with the exchange.

They soon arrived at the Svalbard vault. The two helicopters that had left earlier in the morning had landed on an area cleared the day before by one of Olsen's special units. The landing area was across from the main entrance to the vault. Ten soldiers were now standing there to help the civilian team to get off the third chopper. In a flash, everybody was standing on the ground. Achilles noticed that there were ten other soldiers stationed on the roof of the vault. He turned to look at the ten soldiers on the ground and realised that five of them were standing close to him; he supposed that they were there to protect him. In the end, he was the highest-ranked person in the group. He glanced at the five soldiers with a serious look and they saluted him.

The military devices were initiated effortlessly and Achilles realised that this was the advantage of the army over civil society. The service always had technology and know-how or the funds to acquire them. Connections were quickly established with the military base at Longyearbyen, where the second-in-command of the Norwegian government was waiting for news, along with a representative of the Nordic Alliance, and the Norwegian police. Achilles wore a wrist computer, the latest product put on the market by Mount View University. It was hooked up with the devices of the senior aides who were working on the case. Martha and Roman also had wrist computers which were also connected to Achilles' computer and to the devices of their scientific colleagues at the ONO headquarters in New York.

Olsen explained that his plan was to have four soldiers enter the vault by sliding down the ropes and have them clear the way from the room in which they landed to the main entrance. Once the way was cleared, he added, the teams were to walk down the tunnel, enter the storage room and take stock of the situation. According to Olsen, the whole mission would take four hours and at two o'clock in the afternoon, they would return to Longyearbyen. Martha expressed the wish to join the military crew that was about to enter the vault via the ropes. Achilles agreed. He then explained to the others that Martha was a deep-water and grotto diver, "the best in the world!" She had led many missions concerned with resolving disputes around rivers and waters claimed by more than one country.

Martha was helped up on the roof where she joined the four soldiers ready to descend into the vault. She immediately went to check the ropes and noticed that all three were hanging down. She spoke aloud pointing her device against the objects she was speaking about so that everybody on the ground, and also those in New York, could follow her actions. Olsen expressed surprise at this piece of information. Speaking to Achilles, he said that the soldiers who had come to the vault to prepare the ground for today's mission had left the third rope rolled up on the pavement of the roof. In the meantime, Martha had started to examine the three ropes by shaking them vigorously. She found one of them to be heavier than the other two. Martha asked the soldiers to pull up the ropes. She then threw down the first of the two ropes hanging next to each other. After a little while, they heard a noise which proved that the rope had hit the floor. She then threw down the second rope which took the same time to produce a similar sound. From this, Martha concluded that the two ropes were of the same length. She then moved across to the east side of the roof and threw the third rope but no sound was heard.

"Either this rope is slightly shorter than the other two or the floor is lower or even underwater!" When she uttered these words everybody felt silent. "We'd better use only the two ropes to the right," she advised the soldiers.

Mainly addressing Achilles, Martha said that Roman might want to join her and the crew and descend into the vault via the ropes; he could take a careful look at the vault's walls and check the floor. Achilles nodded, then speaking to Olsen and the others, he explained that Roman was an expert on all kind of materials and that he could tell you exactly what type of stuff had been used to build houses, bridges, streets, spaceships and laboratory products, simply by looking at them. Olsen gave orders for Roman to be lifted up on the roof and in less than ten minutes after his joining Martha and the soldiers, they all descended into the vault by using only two ropes. As soon as they reached the floor of the vault, Roman and Martha moved to the east side of the room, where they supposed the third rope was hanging down. They immediately noticed that there was a hole in the ground and that the rope was ending in water.

"Heavens!" Roman cried while checking out the hole. "What a diabolical construction!" As the devices of those standing outside the vault were connected to the soldiers' body cameras, everybody could see the hole in the ground very clearly, illuminated as it was by the strong light produced by military torches.

"Look at it," Martha said moving closer to the hole, "it is deep, deep water."

"Hm, it looks scary!" Achilles echoed.

"Remember, the biochemist Ananda Barty in 1970?" Roman said addressing Achilles.

"General American Electric, 1970," Achilles immediately replied, "Barty genetically enhanced bacteria to make them metabolise crude oil. Those bacteria were later used to clean up oil spills in Alaska and the Gulf of Mexico."

"We may have a similar story here," Roman offered, "the only difference would be that the bacteria used to cut this hole seem capable of metabolising stones, bricks, mortar, and whatever other material used to build the vault!" Roman's voice was excited but none of what he was saying was of any comfort to the Norwegians.

Olsen turned to Achilles and felt a sense of admiration for him and his people. He was glad he had followed Achilles' advice so far, for what was happening in the vault of Svalbard seemed so different from everything he knew about threats and security. He worked with weapons, Achilles and his people worked with knowledge.

The senior members of GAIC were following the events on remote view.

"Hey George," said Achilles, "what do you think of this?" Then turning to Olsen and the others, Achilles explained that George Lee was a geologist with expertise in soil and rock formations.

"Hm," replied George, "I wonder where those bacteria were manufactured if indeed we are dealing with genetically manipulated bacteria."

"Meher," Achilles said addressing another senior expert in his New York team, "why don't you try to find out if General American Electric has sold Barty's patents or research protocols or if they or anyone else are conducting similar experiments or if they know of someone working on bacteria?"

Achilles then explained to Olsen that Meher Khatri was a geneticist who had previously worked at a university in Massachusetts where bacteria were used to solve technological problems.

"I will go to Boston tomorrow," Meher replied, "and start making some preliminary inquiries and once the theft of the Svalbard's seeds is made public, I'll do some more targeted research."

Martha suddenly recalled having recently read about the discovery of an unusual new mollusc that could bore holes in stones and grind all kind of rocks. She mentioned this to the others. "It's called Lithoredo Abatanica and lives in the deep waters of some rivers in the Philippines but I'm not sure it could live in icy waters like these unless genetically enhanced. I will follow up on this."

The news that bacteria might have been used to cut a hole in the pavement of the vault clearly shocked Olsen but he was not totally convinced that there were bacteria capable of destroying the vault. "If this was true," he said, "weaponised bacteria could destroy the whole world, nothing would be safe, no bridge, no building, no bunker." He spoke in the language of the military.

"Genetically modified bacteria can only survive in the environment for which they have been manufactured. The bacteria that metabolised crude oil, died after the oil spills were resolved and other genetically modified bacteria have a built-in mechanism of self-destruction that kicks in after a set deadline," replied Meher from the remote connection of the ONO office.

"But it could take years to eat up the vault," added the colonel.

"Wouldn't bet on that," said George.

"Perhaps George should join us here." Roman said to Achilles.

An immediate decision was made for George to come to Longyearbyen as soon as possible.

"But how do you stop such bacteria?" Olsen asked in a tense voice. No one was able to give him an answer. Turning to Martha, an impatient colonel asked if anyone could have entered the vault from the hole and as if wanting to increase his own frustration, he added, "Could a submarine come close enough to this hole?"

Martha hesitated. She knew that she would have to examine the hole more carefully and discuss its structure with some deep-water and grotto divers. In the end, they were dealing with icy water where no humans could easily survive without special technology. She waited before answering to see if Achilles was going to stop her but as he kept silent, she concluded that he was happy for her to go ahead.

"A submarine would have to stay at some depth but I think that it could get close enough to the shore to make it possible for some divers to reach the vault by using underwater scooters and then swim to the hole and enter the vault. They would need special swimsuits, though, of the kind that only the military has."

Olsen rolled his eyes. It seemed that the vault of Svalbard was going to become his greatest problem. The government representatives back at the Longyearbyen military base felt a sense of deep fear growing slowly into the size of a political glacier advancing toward the country. No one seemed in the mood to comment on the events that were unfolding. Unexpectedly, the icy water beneath the hole emitted a sound that resembled a soft cry.

"Shit," said the soldier Sandvig turned to Larsen, "had we used the third rope to get into the vault on the day the vandalism was discovered, we'd be dead by now." Everybody sympathised with them.

Olsen asked the military team to clear the way to the main entrance. The soldiers, followed by Martha and Roman, moved toward the exit, they opened it and walked toward a small hall where they found themselves facing a blocked passage. The soldiers removed the stones that blocked the way and after crossing the threshold, with Martha and Roman walking behind, they reached a short corridor at the end of which light was visible. They soon realised that the main entrance was not too far away and, more importantly, that there were no polar bears around. A quick walk and they were finally standing outside. Olsen, still visibly upset about the waterhole, and generally nervous about the weather, checked the time and declared that the mission had to be over in two hours to avoid getting caught in the cold weather of the North Pole.

Chapter 10

The two groups walked down the tunnel that led to the storage hall. The tunnel resembled a tube whose internal walls were covered with a protective layer of glass fibres.

"There's no risk that brick-and-mortar eating bacteria could ever destroy this fibre although they could destroy the construction around it," Roman said making the government's representative look at him alarmed. Achilles turned to Åke as if suddenly struck by his silence. He noticed that Åke was observing everything, taking in every bit of information as if he was reconstructing a scene that would reveal unusual things to him. His expertise was not science, and he never spoke about using scientific methods. Åke was interested in how perception influenced people's choices and their inclusion or exclusion of facts. He sensed Achilles' look and returned it with a smile.

"I'm working hard," he said to Achilles.

They walked fast and soon found themselves in front of the doors of the storage hall, which were all open. Achilles, Martha, and Roman fixed their eyes on the second and third door. As Adam had predicted, only two-thirds of the second door opened. It also opened from the left to the right. The third door in contrast opened from the right to the left and its door panel too opened only to two-thirds. This meant that one-third of door two and one-third of door three remained inaccessible.

No one seemed to notice that the two doors did not open completely. Achilles concluded that the generous size of the doors was probably the reason why people missed that detail. Achilles, Martha, and Roman admired the clever plan that in this way had created a fifth door but they also realised that without Adam's hint they too would probably have failed to notice the trick. Achilles knew that Olsen and the other officials needed to be informed about the fifth door and pondered whether he should share his knowledge on their return to Longyearbyen. At the same time, though, he wished for more proofs to back up the thesis of a hidden door and hoped that Adam would soon be able to find out how to open it. What could be hidden inside? This question never left his mind.

They now entered the storage hall and noticed that it consisted of several rooms, all varying in size for some were large and some others of smaller dimensions. Each room had an inscription above the entrance. A few rooms had been left untouched, particularly those storing seeds of mountain flowers, while other storage rooms were partially empty. The room with the inscription 'Humanity's Basic Seeds' above its entrance had been depleted, and so had the storage room containing seeds derived from the basic ones. Empty was also the storage room that contained seeds of protein-rich roots that grew in Africa, in the mountain regions of South America and in the Asian forests. The seed collections and classifications put together by scientists over a period of many years had been destroyed, perhaps irremediably, by this unprecedented attack. Scattered seeds on the floor created a sad impression as if somebody had contemptuously abandoned pieces of human history. It seemed the thieves knew which storage room to target and which seeds to steal. It also appeared obvious to everyone that whoever had stolen the seeds must have worn gloves and protective clothing, which meant that it would be very difficult to recreate a crime scene in traditional ways. It was in consideration of this possibility that Achilles had included Åke in the mission, hoping he might see things that others, himself included, might not.

Achilles had observed Åke examine the doors attentively, then enter the storage rooms and pay close attention to the walls, doorframes, and floor. He saw him bend down to observe the seeds on the floor, study the broken seed containers, look at the shelves that had intentionally been crashed against the floor. Åke wondered why anyone would want to waste time on the shelves when all the seeds were neatly stored in their glass containers. He then looked up and checked the ceiling. It appeared that some of the thieves had tried to break it, an unsuccessful attempt because the hall's ceiling seemed to be of the same resistant material that was covering the tunnel walls.

Everybody was intent on assessing the damages done to the seed collections when soldiers stationed outside the vault informed Colonel Olsen that the weather was rapidly changing, which made him ask everybody to return to the helicopters. They left the storage rooms and walked up the tunnel toward the main entrance. Halfway through the tunnel, Achilles decided to stop and take a picture of the doors from a distance, and it was then that he noticed Åke's absence. He called out his name aloud and Åke immediately came out of the hall and joined Achilles in a flash. Struck by the speed of that action, Achilles turned his inscrutable look toward Åke, who in noticing it said, "Fast, eh." They caught up with the others and soon they were outside the vault. The weather had indeed deteriorated and it was now necessary to get back to Longyearbyen as quickly as possible.

The helicopter pilots were ready to take-off. The soldiers, except for the ones protecting Achilles and the other civilians, boarded two of the helicopters which started ascending. The team that was still on the ground was walking towards the third helicopter, the soldiers ahead and the civilians immediately following them. Achilles, who was taking pictures whenever he saw a scene to be documented, was last. He was moving quickly when Senorita's drawing unexpectedly came to mind, and as if struck by a sixth sense, he stopped and turned around. He noticed that six polar bears with three offspring had come out of the water and were now walking along the shore. The bears were only fifty yards away. In perceiving that Achilles had stopped, everybody came to a halt and, turning, noticed the bears.

"Don't breathe," said the officer standing next to Olsen. It was obvious to everyone that should the bears attack them, there would be casualties, because the soldiers would not be fast enough to run from their position to where Achilles stood and use their weapons to protect the group. It was at this point that the smallest bear stopped to look at the group of people, and Achilles fancied that he was looking at him. Then it started running ahead of the other bears and having reached the roaring water, it happily dived into it making the other bears follow it and indulge in its play.

Chapter 11

They finally arrived at the Longyearbyen military base where plans were made to return the vault on the following day. Achilles and Olsen, however, would remain at the base and meet representatives of the Norwegian government and the Nordic Alliance. Åke, Martha, Roman and George, who was expected in the evening, would go to the vault along with five of Olsen's soldiers, two military scientists and the Norwegian police. Together they would carry out further inspections, complete some forensic data collection, and other works related to securing the site and closing the main entrance. Once all the plans were finalised, Achilles, Martha, Roman, and Åke were taken to the Svalbard hotel. Achilles suggested an hour's break before regrouping for dinner. He was eager to hear what Åke had to say about the first mission. He had been cautious and quiet all day, and to Achilles, this could only mean that he either saw nothing that others had not also seen or that he saw a lot but could not share his impressions while on the mission.

When they finally sat down for dinner, Roman immediately started to talk about the bacteria. Should his first suspicion about the presence of genetically enhanced bacteria be correct, he said, massive help would be needed to fix the problem. Achilles, still sceptical about bacteria been used in the vault, wondered why anyone would use bacteria if it was so easy to blow up the entrance.

"Would not the transport of such bacteria and all that is connected to such action, have cost more than building the golden gate?"

Martha and Roman agreed and admitted that they did not see any real benefit in the creation of bacteria capable of eating up the vault unless they were part of a design whose importance was now escaping them. They were careful not to mention the invisible door because Åke was not yet aware of it. Achilles, now eager to know if he had seen anything unusual, turned to him and asked for his impressions. Åke took his time before answering. What he said, however, removed all the doubts that his silence had caused. I hope, he said, that you paid attention to the floor of the storage hall and the tunnel, to which the others replied that they had not. It was his strong opinion that the thieves must have left hastily, that "something must have made them leave abruptly since there were seeds all over the place". He was also troubled by the fact that only the shelves that had stood against the walls of the storage room had been torn down which seemed to suggest that the thieves were after something that had to do with the walls. And of course, he found it unusual that the electronic square on the third door was placed on the right-hand side and not on the left as was the case with the other three doors.

"What are your conclusions?" asked Achilles secretly admiring Åke's observations.

"There must be something in between the walls," answered Åke immediately, "and I believe that it is not seeds."

"A hidden chamber for something dangerous?" Achilles suggested.

"Or precious," replied Åke without hesitation.

"What makes you say this?" Achilles inquired.

"If Roman's thesis about the bacteria is correct, then it's clear to me that there's a lot at stake."

Achilles made no comment but Åke's answer made him circumspect because it showed that Åke was using the method of probability rather than unusuality. He wondered what the reason for this change of style could be and made a mental note about it. He looked at Martha and Roman to see how they reacted to Åke's answer but he found them inscrutable. Suddenly, the door opened and George entered. They all greeted him warmly, and another chair was added to the table so that he could join them for a good meal. The conversation now changed to small talk with George speaking about his flight and then switching to general topics. They spent one more hour together until Åke sensing that the ONO people wanted to speak about issues that might be classified, decided that it was time for him to leave.

Hereafter, George instantly asked for more particulars about the mission to which Martha and Roman replied with eagerness. It was evident from their way of talking that they admired Åke's work. They found his observations about the shelves and the doors quite impressive. Contrary to how Achilles felt, they were not worried at his dodging the question about a hidden chamber, which in their view showed Åke's attempt to buy some more time before committing himself. Martha suspected him of being a perfectionist. "Like all of us," she added smiling sweetly.

It was now George's turn to contribute. He had made enquiries about research on bacteria and so had Meher who was currently in Massachusetts for this purpose. He suspected that some bacteria used in research might have been smuggled out of industrial and academic laboratories, and it could well be that some of those enhanced bacteria were now in the wrong hands. Should bacteria have escaped or been smuggled out of research facilities, George concluded, it would be hard to know their whereabouts. Suddenly changing topic, George passed on a message from Adam. Unfortunately, Adam had not understood yet how algorithm architecture can hide places, and therefore was heading to Mount View University to find out what his former colleagues knew.

As they were talking, Meher got in contact with Achilles from Cambridge, America's A.I. and genetics incubator. She was hoping, she said, to meet with some former colleagues to find out the latest developments in bacteria research. Before getting off the conversation, Meher informed him that she would soon travel to India to visit her parents and that on that occasion she might try to meet professor Barty at the University of Calcutta.

As the evening was winding down, Achilles told his aides that the director-general was going to release a media communiqué about the theft of the Svalbard seeds on the coming Friday at five o'clock. They had intentionally chosen the last day of the working week in order to gain some more time before the press conference set for Monday afternoon. He then reminded them to attend the Monday meeting he had scheduled for nine o'clock and to which he had invited the senior and junior staff working on the case. He then mentioned that after tomorrow's meeting with Olsen he would return to Oslo to collect his belongings and fly back to New York via London. Here, he would meet his mother and uncle and some friends who worked on food and deserts. "By Monday morning, we will all be back in New York." Martha, George, and Roman looked at him smiling. They knew that, when Achilles spoke of friends, he sometimes also meant people who were in the know about things he needed.

On the following morning at five, they were collected by a military crew in an army vehicle and taken to Longyearbyen. Achilles met Olsen and other governmental representatives while the others went to the vault to further investigate the site. Åke promised to get in touch with Achilles over the weekend. He seemed to be after something but Achilles did not ask for explanations; he was glad though that Åke was showing some signs of optimism. Achilles asked Martha, George, and Roman to stay in contact throughout the day and keep him informed about their impressions.

When Achilles entered the main office of the military base, he immediately saw that Olsen was not in good form. On enquiring about the reasons, Olsen, after taking a deep breath, admitted that he felt overwhelmed by the events.

"I'm used to fighting enemies who are like me. I can't fight genetically manipulated bacteria."

"Just imagine that they are the product of someone, hm, a laboratory soldier, if you like," suggested Achilles.

While they were speaking, the government's representatives, along with the police and the secret service joined them in Olsen's office. Achilles asked for some updates from their perspectives. The Norwegian government was deeply worried about how to inform its people of the theft of the seeds and how to reassure the country that everything was under control when in fact, little with regard to the vault seemed to be under control. Achilles told them that on the following day, the ONO director-general would issue a media release about the theft of the seeds and that the Norwegian government might want to inform Norway's political and military partners before then. He also suggested that, given the high risks implicated in the theft, flights to Svalbard should be monitored and if necessary, the presence of tourists limited. Achilles let them also know that he was going to leave in the afternoon but that the ONO staff would be in the vault for the whole of Friday. George in particular, continued Achilles, wanted to look more closely at the glaciers, soil and rocks in the areas around the Svalbard vault. His scientific aides would return to New York on Saturday and he would send Olsen copies of their reports. Olsen and the others seemed worried to see him go. Especially, the colonel had come to appreciate the importance of ONO, and he took a particular and lengthy leave from Achilles by mixing personal and professional issues. Olsen clearly admired Achilles and his ability to galvanise people and make them work for good causes. He had also noticed Achilles' ability to resist all kind of political and moral pressures, no matter where they came from while looking for common solutions. But no matter how great his appreciation of Achilles was, Olsen would soon come to understand what it really meant to work with him. Achilles was far beyond anything the world had ever seen. He was the king of informed consent.

Chapter 12

When Achilles touched down at Heathrow Airport, the ONO director-general had just put out a press communiqué informing the world of the theft of the Svalbard seeds. The news immediately reverberated through the media. Achilles went to his uncle's residence outside London. His mother and uncle William now understood why Achilles had come from Oslo and not from New York. When the day before he had informed them of his arrival from Norway, his mother and uncle had wondered about the reason for the detour. His mother secretly entertained the hope that Achilles might have a special person in Oslo but the news about the theft of the seeds made her realise that the reason for his son's travels were work-related. She mentioned this to Achilles when they were together at dinner, making her son smile sweetly. It was her personal way of letting him know that she did not like to see him single. His uncle was less worried about that, although he threw in an affectionate remark about the problems of living alone. During their dinner, they spoke about various matters relating to Achilles' cousins. They were expected to join them for lunch the following day. Achilles liked the idea of having them around and looked forward to two happy days ahead. Then, unable to hold back his worries, turned to the possible reasons behind the theft of the seeds.

"Have you come across news about droughts and food deserts?"

His uncle crossed his arms and said that, yes, he had recently discussed issues associated with droughts with the British government, and other governments within the commonwealth, for which he worked as a political consultant. Before taking on this role, he had been one of the first negotiators to work in the system of informed consent and had been instrumental in making Achilles decide to work for GAIC as a young graduate and during his doctoral studies.

"From what I have recently seen," continued his uncle, "there have been several cases of famine in areas that never used to have food problems, even in regions where there is no lack of water or farmland."

"That's strange," commented Achilles' mother, "why is this?"

"We don't know," said William, "how do you view these trends, Achilles?"

Achilles answered that this was an issue he needed to explore a bit more before making any comments.

"Do you have any idea who could want the global seeds?"

"Oh, if you ask me," replied his uncle, "there are many people and governments that would pay millions for those seeds, now that oil has no bargaining power anymore."

"I have recently read a novel," said his mother, "a dystopian novel, I should say, in which the author imagines a world where all basic seeds have been confiscated and the production of food globally centralised, so governments have to negotiate about how many seeds they can get and how much food they can produce." In saying this, she stood up and left the room only to return a few minutes later, holding in her hand the book she had just mentioned. She handed it to Achilles, who flipped through it quickly. At length, his attention was caught by the author's name, which he read out aloud, 'Fami Ne'. He paused briefly and then cried out, "Ingenious!" His mother and uncle wanted to know what was intriguing him so much.

"If you put the first name and the family name together, you get the word famine."

Achilles looked at the title, *Love's Over*. "Hm!"

"You see," said his mother, "anyone holding this book would spontaneously think that it's a book about love, and at first, the story does seem to be about relationships gone astray and sex not being forthcoming. A few pages into the book, however, the style and tone change and become somehow suggestive, making you hold onto it because the story is captivating and you want to see how all ends up. It's a tricky book," she concluded.

"Where did you buy it?" Achilles asked.

"It was sent to me for a book review."

As a writer, Achilles' mother was often asked by journals, newspapers, and literary magazines to review books for them, which she did with great pleasure. She was such an outstanding reviewer that she had more books sent to her for review than she could possibly read. She usually picked the ones that had a direct appeal to her.

"Sent to you by whom?"

"By a journal called *Desert*."

"I've never heard of it," said Achilles.

"Oh, I've seen several copies of that journal lie around at the foreign office," said William.

"Who is publishing it?" asked Achilles surprised.

"Hm… not sure about that," said his uncle.

"I wonder if Claire is familiar with this journal," Achilles wondered.

"Apropos Claire," interjected his mother, "why don't you invite her for lunch tomorrow? We'd love to see her, John, and the children. It's been a while since we had them over."

Claire and Achilles went to school and university together, and although Achilles had many friends, Claire had always been one of his favourites. Her parents were commercial law consultants or what used to be called lawyers, always too busy with work to really be able to look after her, so sometimes Claire came and stayed with Achilles. Her parents called every night to kiss her good night via their devices, and they always spoke softly with her for almost an hour. Achilles' mother found them sensible in their interactions with Claire, whom they came to see once a week. They felt bad about their work addiction but they also knew that their daughter was happy where she was.

Following up on his mother's suggestion, Achilles sent Claire an invitation for the next day's family lunch, which Claire accepted. Achilles' family was large. When he turned five and a half, his mother moved to her brother to live in the old London family house where they were just now. The house was large and could easily accommodate two families. Achilles grew up with his three cousins: Anne, Kathrin, and Henry. His cousins had built their families. Achilles found their partners as lovely as their children. Anne had married Rosemary, a girl from the north of England, and together they now had a girl called Joy and a boy called Daniel. Kathrin had married her school sweetheart whom she met when she was twelve. They had a boy called Alex. And then there was Henry who lived together with his partner Renzo. They had two boys, Constantin and Moritz and a girl, Lance.

When on the following day the cousins and their families finally arrived, the joyful tumult caused by hugs, kisses, and loud greetings could be heard throughout the house. Achilles first listened to the stories of the children, each of them had happiness but also worries to relate, which he tried to help them overcome by suggesting some ideas and plans that could appeal to the young. He had brought each of them a present from Svalbard, a polar bear made of lucent glass. He had chosen a different colour for each child, and Achilles noticed how the children were holding the bears in their hands and fixing their eyes on the beautiful glass. So different were these presents from the ones that children were receiving these days.

After the pleasure of playing and chatting with his young cousins, Achilles turned to the adults. They too had stories of success and failure to tell but as a whole, their understanding of what was going on in the world was good. Achilles did not agree with everything they said but learned a lot about their ideas. When Claire, John and their two boys Alessandro and Giovanni finally arrived, the family circle was complete. They were received with warmth, although Anne, one of the cousins, complained that they had not seen the children for quite a long time, to which Claire replied with a promise to visit more often in the future. The lunch was a real feast. Uncle William had ordered food from a restaurant down the road, and the table was soon full of dishes from various cuisines. And the dessert was zuppa inglese.

After lunch, adults and children went to the local park to take part in a children's festival. Achilles stayed behind with Claire and John. They told him that they were familiar with the journal *Desert* but not with the book by Fami Ne. Claire and John also informed him that in a week's time they were going to attend a conference organised by the Blue People, the Tuaregs of the Sahara. The Tuaregs were a Berber ethnic confederation that had decided to open a small university called The University of the Desert. The Tuaregs had become more sedentary and over the years, their settlements had led to the establishment of the Blue City, the capital of the Tuareg confederation. Not that they had renounced their traditional nomadic lifestyle, which in fact continued undisturbed. The university had already attracted some outstanding academics and initiated research start-ups about the desert. It hosted an annual conference that brought knowledge and ideas to the confederation, a tangible sign of the university's innovative strategy.

This year's conference was about changes in the desert and of the desert. Claire said that Amastan Badis Hammadit, the rector of the university, was a chemist who had studied in England. The name sounded familiar to Achilles but he could not recall any direct connection with him. Claire added that Amastan Badis was now married to Gwafa Illi Tin Hinan, a Tuareg princess and descendant of the ancient Queen of the Hoggar through their matrilineal lineage. Gwafa Illi's mother was the current Queen but because of her prolonged illness, her daughter acted as a regent. Like her husband, Gwafa Illi had studied at the same university as Claire and Achilles and had degrees in archaeology and mathematics. At this point, John, who was also an archaeologist, entered the conversation and explained that the conference would take place in the Sahara and it would include only a selected number of people.

"What is the purpose of the conference?" Achilles was trying to figure out if knowledge about the desert could help him solve his problem with the missing seeds.

"Gwafa Illi's grandfather and late father," said John, "had discovered several faults in the central desert; they carried out excavations to determine what caused the faults to form but their work led to nothing till five years ago, Gwafa Illi had noticed some new faults within a one-mile radius from the old ones." John's voice sounded excited and his eyes shone.

"She immediately began some new excavations in the area and invited me and two other international archaeologists to take part in her desert expeditions; the two other scientists were a mountaineer from Switzerland and an expert on water architecture from Holland. We joined the excavations and noticed that the desert had been sucked in, which made us suspect that there could be a cave beneath the faults or perhaps more than just a cave. Gwafa Illi wanted more excavations and promised to start work as soon as possible."

John went on to say that thereafter Gwafa Illi had been pregnant twice and now had a girl and a boy who were four and three, respectively. It was during this period that the princess and her husband had established The University of the Desert. Their relentless and outstanding work led to the organisation of several successful conferences and the establishment of the academic journal Desert; all these activities brought an enormous reputation to the place.

John concluded by saying that Gwafa Illi and Amastan were now ready to resume excavations, which they were going to discuss with him and others at the upcoming conference.

Claire further explained that the scientists studying that part of the desert had found some wet spots around the faults that seemed to suggest the presence of water, while the appearance of some plants, she added, also seemed to reinforce this idea. The vegetation had grown considerably and it was now generally believed within the scientific community that an effort should be made to find out why.

Achilles asked them to keep him informed about the developments in the desert before their conversation turned to mundane topics. After chatting for some time about friends and acquaintances, however, Achilles felt impatient to relate, and they to hear, what had happened in Svalbard. He recounted his visit to the vault trying to keep out some of the classified bits but his next questions let worries transpire that his friends, by being scientists, picked up immediately.

"Have you ever heard of any scientific research that genetically enhances bacteria or microbes to make them digest hard materials?"

They had. They could tell him that the number of scientific articles on enhanced bacteria and microbes had increased exponentially. Not only archaeologists but also palaeontologists, said John, were interested in understanding if bacteria could be used to remove stones and other material nested deep in the geological earth strata.

"Some of today's young laboratory scientists are bold and fearless but unfortunately, their eyes are all for results and none for the consequences of their activities," said Claire.

"Hm." Achilles' monosyllable revealed his apprehension. "Will you let me know if you pick up something on this issue?"

"Of course," said Claire.

Time had passed quickly. The others returned from the children's festival, and now tea and coffee and more cakes and biscuits, warm food and drinks, toasts and cheese were shared by all in happiness, till the moment of separation arrived. The adieus took some time but in the end, calm returned. Achilles decided to dive into the heated water of the swimming pool behind the house where he swam until exhaustion. He spent the remaining hours before his departure reading and playing billiards with his uncle. His mother joined them, now and then, to announce who had arrived home and to pass on their renewed hugs and kisses. When he retired to prepare for his flight back to New York, Achilles felt the importance of the family. *The only institution that neither state nor work will ever destroy*, he thought to himself. He admired the way the world's oldest institution had managed to rejuvenate itself with the help of all the new multi gender constellations that were now also part of his own family.

Chapter 13

Thanks to the fleet of Sir Entrepreneur, Achilles was back in New York in less than two hours and reached his home before midnight. He quickly unpacked his luggage to retrieve the small presents he had bought for Juanita's children from his bag. He noticed that Carlos had left a welcome note: he had prepared some warm food and filled his fridge. Achilles was grateful for the friendly gesture. He was happy to be back but felt nervous about the problems relating to the Svalbard vault. Monday morning arrived quickly. At six in the morning, Achilles was already in his office where he found Romeo waiting for him with one of his restorative breakfasts. Many of the staff were already at work and passed by to say hello. "You have been missed!" was their returning message. The director-general joined him in the GAIC café, visibly pleased to have him back. He wanted, he said, to address the upcoming meeting.

The meeting started on time. The director-general was the first to speak. He reminded everybody of their responsibility to carry out their tasks sensibly and to stay alert. He added that the Norwegians had asked US Defence for assistance in dealing with the problem of the waterhole found in one of the vault's rooms and that Martha, George, and Roman would brief the meeting about all issues related to the theft.

"It seems," he said, "that the Norwegians have not noticed anything about the number of doors, not sure about Defence though." He hoped that Adam would be able to say more about the issue.

He had also conducted some inquiries into the security system at the vault. Technological safety and security were one of the director-general's fields of expertise. The firm that had originally installed the security system of the Svalbard vault was bought up by another firm immediately after the completion of the construction works; this later firm was itself subsequently acquired by another firm and was later sold to a third firm. A couple of years later, the Norwegian firm that was currently overseeing the security of the vault, bought it.

As he was listening to the director-general, Achilles was pleased to discover consistency between this information and the information shared by Colonel Olsen about the security firm. The director-general added that the present security firm had the safety plan of the vault, and yesterday they had contacted him to inform him that they intended to conduct a test under the supervision of the Norwegian government. The director-general concluded by stating that the security firm had confirmed that there were four doors on the plan and that four doors were originally built on site.

It was now Achilles' turn. After addressing some preliminaries related to security, he invited those who had to action tasks or had been on missions to give a short report about their findings. As always, Achilles let his junior secretaries start. Lucillo had been in Houston and had talked with people at NASA. Apparently, the agency was not currently conducting any projects related to food, although settlements on Mars were in preparation. Parys had visited various people around the country who were known for storing vast quantities of food. Some were survivalists who collected food in preparation for natural catastrophes while others were everyday people terrified by climate change. Unfortunately, Parys had not managed to secure a meeting with a collector who the others kept referring to for being the most experienced in the storage of difficult material. He was said to be a microbiologist and an expert in marine flora such as Arctic moss and Seaweeds from the North Pole. People said that he owned a big hangar in some deserted part of Detroit where his natural library, as he referred to it, was allegedly stored.

Finally, Annabelle reported that she had followed up some discussions about climate change and drought and that this research made her discover a new journal called *Desert*. She added that the journal was published by the rector of The University of the Desert, owned by the Blue People, adding for those who were not familiar with the term that the Blue people were the Tuaregs. Annabelle further explained that the journal had invited a number of selected scientists to attend a conference in the Sahara Desert and that she had asked permission to participate in the conference as a PhD student. Her application was, however, rejected. She reapplied as a member of ONO at which point the conference organisers asked her to specify the agency she was working with. When she informed them that she was in GAIC and reporting to Achilles, they accepted her application. Everybody expressed appreciation for the work done by the junior staff but only Achilles understood the importance of Annabelle's doings.

He sensed that the organisers of the conference wanted to involve him.

Once the juniors had completed their reports, the seniors presented theirs. Adam was the first to speak. He had been at Silicon Valley and had met the owners of the IT firm that had developed the secret program Defence had invited him to review for them. The only bit he could reveal concerning the program, said Adam, was its name *Visibility*. Continuing his account, Adam said that the Silicon Valley firm was now aware that he had tested it on an object that was classified within ONO which precluded him from revealing the nature of the object to the firm. Adam observed that since the theft of the seeds was now public knowledge, the IT firm and Defence might be wondering if he had tested the program on the Svalbard vault. He was, however, not worried about that because they would not know how to go ahead with such a test. Adam continued his reporting by saying that he then went to Mount View University to meet some of his former colleagues. As there was a technology conference taking place on campus, other experts from Cupertino and Redmond Universities attended the meeting along with mathematicians and biochemical nano-robotic experts from the Massachusetts Institute of A.I. Without Adam revealing his problem or them enquiring about it, he asked them questions about algorithm research.

Adam went on to say that some people, including some of his former colleagues, were working on so-called complex algorithms, also known as CAs. These were sets of rules and designs never seen before that allowed for problem-solving and machine learning in a sophisticated way. Adam said that while he was listening to the scientists, he realised that CAs could have an enormous impact on humans. By being himself a computer and algorithm expert, Adam declared, he knew that the word 'sophisticated' was being used in his community to indicate novelty that was not yet totally understood. He had asked his former colleagues about the nature of CAs and the answers were not always reassuring. Some considered these algorithms to be potentially harmful. But there were also CAs that could also support humans and serve their interests. Adam went on to say that many of the scientists working on algorithms and A.I. were trying to anticipate the risks associated with CAs in order to be able to mitigate any unwanted effects. He said that it was a battle between the best minds in the field. After a brief pause, during which he appeared to be visibly nervous, Adam concluded that he had not yet managed to figure out how to open the hidden door but he was working on it and getting closer to a solution. Adam's account made everybody feel a sense of urgency and a desire to move onto the next stage of the case.

Martha, George, and Roman now gave their reports. They had mainly focused on the waterhole in the east room of the vault and noticed that it had expanded several inches every day, which seemed to confirm their first assessment that some sort of caustic bacteria were destroying the vault. They also stated that, at such speed, the whole floor of the east room would be gone in a couple of months. Further inspections of other floors within the vault, for example along the tunnel and in the storage hall revealed wet spots. In some other parts of the building, they noticed that the floor had caved in, opening up the possibility that genetically modified bacteria, joined by natural microbes, which they suspected to be highly corrosive, could be spreading beneath the whole vault and speeding up the erosion process. Martha, George, and Ramon also observed that the Norwegian government and military had allowed their scientists to enter the vault to examine the floors of the whole vault. A report about their inspection of the vault was expected shortly. Martha and Roman declared that they would carry out further laboratory tests to identify the type of bacteria and microbes around the waterhole and perhaps call on the expertise of some of their former colleagues and friends.

Meher now followed with her account. She had just returned from Boston where she had met with several people working in the field of genetic enhancement. To help Meher quench her thirst for knowledge about bacteria, Forrow Dickson, a former friend from college, had organised a dinner party to which she had invited the best researchers working in this scientific domain in the Cambridge-Boston area. Meher explained that Forrow was a scientist with 'GenNew', an emerging firm in Cambridge devoted to building organic machines. Meher spoke about the geneticists and biologists attending the party, some of whom she described as being very charismatic. Achilles made a separate mental note about this piece of information. For the main part of the evening, Meher continued, not much was said about bacteria until somebody mentioned forbidden research. It was Sam Bethe, a friend of Furrow, whose job was to investigate breaches of research protocols and norms at various medical and scientific centres. Sam was after a controversial article that had been published in a shady journal called *New Nature*. The authors of the article, who were down only with their initials, described an experiment with a new breed of genetically enhanced bacteria that could metabolise hard materials. They tested their bacteria against three objects, one of which remained undisclosed, which made people in the field, Sam included, wonder about the authenticity of the research. Yet, the topic was of such interest that it attracted the attention of several research centres. When scientists tried to retrieve the article, however, they realised that it had disappeared from the web. Other guests who were listening to the conversation said that the journal was on *Instant Sensory*, a platform that accepted postings that self-destroyed sixty minutes after their uploading. *Instant Sensory* intentionally accepted only forbidden research, that is, research that was breaking scientific and ethical rules, and possibly violating informed consent. Meher concluded her account by saying that even five minutes on that platform would be enough to reach the people you wanted.

After everybody's report was heard, Achilles summarised the main issues and shared his plans. He spoke about his meeting at the military base of Longyearbyen and informed them that the Norwegian government had claimed the right to enter the vault whenever necessary without the permission of ONO, despite ONO being the legal guarantor of the vault. The reason for the Norwegian request, Achilles said, was national security. Achilles further explained that in consultation with the director-general, he did not oppose the wish of the Norwegian government to go into the vault. But, he said, he had reminded its representatives and their allies that if they wanted to fight a threat, they first had to be clear about the nature of that threat, which in the case of the vault might not follow a traditional script. Achilles also said that he had let governments and their agencies understand that they needed

ONO to solve this crime because of the new type of logic involved.

In the light of the latest developments, Achilles concluded, it was now necessary to adapt to what was happening. He asked Parys to return to Detroit to find out what his elusive collector knew about unusual storage places. He advised Lucillo to put NASA aside for now and instead focus on research about melting glaciers and its effects on land and people. In concluding the meeting, Achilles urged everybody to continue to stay focused and work for informed consent.

In the afternoon, ONO gave a press conference. The director-general, together with his aides and secretaries, addressed the media. Achilles attended the media conference but made no comments. The journalists asked many questions but in sensing that answers were not always forthcoming, they wondered whether all information relating to the stolen seeds had been released to which the director-general replied, without entering into specifics, that there were still a few classified matters he was not at liberty to talk about. This was enough to send the media into a spin with journalists and media experts now interested in starting their own investigation into the theft of the seeds. Achilles had always worked well with the media, which in his view had the freedom and duty to keep people updated on important events to help them form opinions based on the best available evidence and information. Faithful to this belief, he had always given Angelo the space to maintain a productive dialogue with the media. Angelo understood how to deal with broad bases and elites, hence no one seemed more suitable to deal with all the media enquiries related to the vault of Svalbard than him.

Chapter 14

On Tuesday morning, Olsen contacted Achilles. They had found a device at the Longyearbyen base that belonged to a former soldier. That soldier had gone to the Svalbard vault with the two crews that failed to file reports about their inspections. The colonel added that on the soldier's device there were only songs and music by a band called *Save the Earth*. The band, he said, was part of a broad ecological and environmental movement that attracted many young followers.

Achilles thanked him for this piece of information. During their conversation, the colonel also mentioned the waterhole in the east side room of the vault hinting that politicians were taking the issue very seriously. He also added that the Norwegian opposition parties, media, and people wanted to know what the ONO director-general had meant by speaking of classified issues during his media conference. Mentioning that patience was running thin in his country when it came to the Svalbard vault, Olsen suggested that something had to be said or done to avoid a political crisis of unknown ramifications. Achilles understood this was an indirect request for help.

"We are working hard," said Achilles, "but we can't take shortcuts. We need to understand as precisely as possible who did what and why, and then we will negotiate a solution."

"How long will it take?"

"Hopefully not too long," he replied, "but don't let politics distract you, and try instead to understand the underlining method, how not just what happened, and once you are closer to that understanding, let's reconvene and discuss what you've found out."

Olsen decided to interpret Achilles' words as an encouragement to follow his military instinct rather than the plans of politicians, and he liked the message.

"How high are the stakes?"

"Very high!" Achilles instantly replied. Then, as if to comfort the colonel who was facing a new type of challenge and failed to receive any serious help from the traditional agencies, Achilles promised to keep him informed about whatever news he could share.

"Is there something I don't know yet?" the colonel asked.

"Yes," said Achilles mortified, "but this is because I don't know yet myself whether we are dealing with an idea or a real problem." Achilles was thinking of the hidden door about which no further information was forthcoming. "But I am hoping to have some news for you soon."

"OK, thanks."

Afterwards, Achilles called an urgent meeting with the four interns who had started a few weeks earlier. He knew them personally but he had not had the time yet to discuss their roles with them. The theft of the seeds, he thought, would be a good opportunity to introduce them into the workings of his office. Ajana, Emily, Fatin, and Luca were carrying out tasks under the direction of Angelo, who had kept them informed about all the relevant facts relating to the theft of the seeds. They were eager to learn and be part of Achilles' team. Their office was next to Angelo's but located on a mezzanine which was suspended in the air and which could only be reached via a mobile platform. When Achilles entered the office assigned to the interns, their faces lit up. He greeted them affectionately but also with a serious look. He had brought them some of Romeo's tasty hot chocolate and they now sat down together. After summarising the major problems relating to the theft of the seeds, Achilles mentioned the music band *Save the Earth.* He soon found that the interns admired it, and although they had differing ideas about the band, they were all appreciative of its videos, songs and performances. The interns found the band 'courageous', an expression that made Achilles stare at them because this was a word he himself used with great parsimony. Achilles asked the interns to explain what it meant to be courageous for a band, and they replied that the band had the courage to show the suffering of the earth and all its creatures. Achilles was touched by this statement and invited his youngest collaborators to let him see and hear one of the performances of the band.

The interns picked a concert from the web that the band had given in New York the year before. Achilles was stunned by the large audience. There were a hundred thousand fans or even more, and all enveloped in a surreal atmosphere. The song chosen by the interns was titled *Cruel.* It started with images of droughts and dying animals. The musicians made their instruments sound like the calls of a herd of cows which at first sounded happy but then increasingly weak and desperate, till they turned into the excruciating sound of dying animals. The front man and girl intensified the animals' cries through their amplifiers. Then the interns showed him a video about birds flying happily over oceans and arriving at their final destination to find only dry ponds where the birds slowly died of fatigue and thirst. Again, the voice of the front singers imitated the twits of dying birds. After these images, the video showed children running over green fields, playing joyfully and then falling on dry soil, crying loudly, crying softly, looking for water, holding tight onto their parents' dead bodies. Achilles found the video devastating and its colours, although magnificent, amplified the sense of total despair, and it also seemed to him that the music cut deeply into your body like a blade that left you physically powerless. Then the interns chose a second video on which the band performed aggressively and played a song called *J'accuse*.

J'accuse!
Earth is dying
Time for fighting
Humans broke the vow
That glued us all
Into creatures of care
With powers to share
Earth is dying
Time for fighting
Human hands have destroyed
What nature on us had bestowed
The duty to sort out
The danger of droughts
Earth is dying

Time for fighting
J'accuse J'accuse
Humans who took
The freedom to kill
Earth and our will

These words were accompanied by music so powerful that the listeners felt disoriented. A third video showed a series of terrifying images of fires and flooded, frozen, deserted places where no life was apparent until a trembling thin hand was seen planting a tiny seed in fertile soil, then a second seed, and another one, at which point the earth became alive with seeds sprouting all over. The music accompanying the images was very potent and the silence that had muted the young audience was suddenly replaced by joyous clapping and cries. Achilles observed that the four interns were captivated by the video but as soon as they noticed his scrutinising look, they smiled at him. Realising that the interns' admiration for the band also revealed the power of the visual over them, Achilles realised that something needed to be said to help them acquire some perspective. He tried to understand their thoughts by asking if in their view the videos and the lyrics were portraying reality as it was. The four interns were cautious in their replies, sensing that Achilles' question was not the result of mere curiosity.

"You see," he said, "a negotiator must always, and I emphasise always, know things as they are, with absolute correctness or at least enough correctness to give the negotiator the certainty that is needed to facilitate consensual decisions among people. And this is important not only to us negotiators but also to the rhetoricians who, as you know, are the ones who craft the conditions for informed consent." The interns were listening with the utmost attention, realising that Achilles was initiating them into the role of the negotiator. They nodded to show that they had understood and thanked him for reminding them of the need to work towards a balance or what Achilles on other occasions had called, the Aristotelian middle.

Achilles now asked the interns to do some work for him. He wanted them to collect all the lyrics and videos of the band, find out where the band had performed during the last two years, and its future concert schedule, particularly when and where the next concert was due. Achilles also asked them to collect as much information as possible about each band member and to retrieve all publicly available data about the leading personalities of the band. "If necessary," he said, "travel to where the band members are living or performing and find out all we need to know about them and their plans." Achilles asked each of them to file a report specific to their research task. There was no need to remind them about their role. He knew that they had understood what was required of them within GAIC. Afterwards, he wished them good luck with their tasks and left.

While he was listening to the band, Achilles wondered why the lyrics of its songs had sounded familiar to him, and soon realised that they reminded him of the book *Love's Over* by Fami Ne. Achilles had read the book while he was staying in London. It was a novella about two lovers, Nature and Humanity. In it, the author described how a beautiful love of interdependence and reciprocal affection turned sour, how neglect followed and violence destroyed their relationship. The book showed Nature losing out to nasty and brutal

Humanity. The book was well written but the empathy it evoked could blind the reader to the ideological message that humans were ruthless rulers. From here, the step to hating all that was human was short. "Perhaps too short for informed consent," Achilles mused.

Once in his office, Achilles grabbed the book by Fami Ne and a box of chocolate bacios and paid a visit to the rhetoricians. The rhetoricians always worked cooperatively with the negotiators but they had ambitions that needed to be checked since they could make the working of informed consent difficult by introducing loose rules. As the top-negotiator, Achilles had power over them. As he entered their office, he found the rhetoricians in their main room and judging from their serious look, they were engaged in some important discussion. They welcomed him very cordially and understood immediately that if he had come to them, it was because he needed something from them. Everyone who has ever witnessed the encounter between negotiators and rhetoricians knows that often, although not always, their friendliness is marked by rhetorical tricks that only an experienced negotiator can manage. They engaged in small talk for a little while, which was a way of testing each other's mood. Achilles noticed that in addition to the seven most senior rhetoricians present in the room, there was one he had never met before. The new rhetorician was introduced as Meme. Achilles admired Meme but also found the features of his face too perfect as if cut with a fine chisel. Achilles asked the rhetoricians if they were familiar with a band called *Save the Earth,* and they answered that they were. Achilles then asked them if they were familiar with the book *Love's Over.* They were. He did not expect more than a simple confirmation; it was in fact an iron rule with rhetoricians to give away as little as possible about their thoughts and opinions. Achilles asked them to start working on the band's messages. "I might soon host a global negotiation and was thinking of asking this band to participate." The rhetoricians nodded. Their head replied, "Whenever you call on us, we'll be ready."

After this exchange, Achilles opened the chocolate box and threw a chocolate bacio to the head rhetorician who caught it in mid-air effortlessly, unwrapped it and discovered inside a little aphorism printed on a delicate paper folded around the chocolate. The rhetorician read it out aloud: "A friend is, as it were, a second self. Marcus Tullio Cicero." Then Achilles made a gesture as if to throw another chocolate to the deputy rhetorician who was sitting opposite him, instead, he threw it to Meme who was sitting two chairs away from the deputy. Meme failed to catch the chocolate. Even before the other rhetoricians could recover from their surprise, Achilles asked Meme in a commanding tone, "What's your expiring date?"

"Exact twenty years from today," Meme replied.

Achilles left the office of the rhetoricians. He had scored a few points against them but had also gained their admiration, which always guaranteed the rhetoricians' loyalty.

Chapter 15

Achilles went to the GAIC café and ordered a refreshing drink. He was sitting leisurely and going through some of the communications and letters he had received recently. One, in particular, attracted his attention because it was a real letter and not a printout from an email inbox. Since hardcopy letters had become a rarity, he turned to it with eagerness and discovered that it was from the 'Coalition of Humanists'. The Coalition was requesting a negotiation to regulate the use of language in the climate change debate and more generally in the environmentalist scene. The authors of the letter complained about the use of expressions such as 'human-made climate change' or 'the human impact on climate' and lamented their indiscriminate use which, in their view, contributed to an escalation of hate against humanity. The signatories of the letter named a list of politically engaged scientists and various groups, including the band *Save the Earth* and the Earth Movement, whose members, in their view, were culpable of embodying a new puritan-like fanaticism. The coalition was asking GAIC to negotiate a common understanding of the climatic problems and help 'stunt the growth of heresy'.

While considering how to respond to the request, Achilles received a communication from the Nordic Alliance. Its chair, Professor Claus Reverber, informed him that the alliance had decided to reward anyone providing information about the seeds; the Alliance was also going to pay a reward of 100 million for the return of all undamaged seeds stolen from the vault of Svalbard. The reward would be in the currency that had the highest value on the day of the return of the seeds. Achilles warned Reverber of the risk of being flooded with false information about the whereabouts of the seeds, he also pointed out that the high reward for the return of the seeds might attract people who acted outside informed consent. Achilles wanted to keep the alliance focused on organising new seed collections rather than trying to get back the stolen ones which, he observed its chair, might have been damaged through their storage in unsuitable places. Reverber remained stubbornly oblivious to all possible problems related to the rewards, which surprised Achilles. Reverber also said that his was just a courtesy communication to Achilles and that the communiqué about the rewards would be issued shortly. Achilles nodded and terminated the conversation. He questioned the motives behind the decision of the Nordic Alliance or perhaps just its chair?

Achilles went to the office of the negotiators, his closest collaborators. He had brought with him the letter from the Coalition of Humanists and after discussing its content with the senior negotiators, he said that he had made up his mind and was ready to call and host a global negotiation to sort out the issues mentioned in the letter and some new ones, particularly those highlighted by the stolen seed. Achilles also discussed with them the reports about the band *Save the*

Earth, which the interns had sent him earlier. He explained that the band was the public face of the Earth Movement and that such movement attracted many teens, particularly those pressing for climate change action. The reports also described the scene around the band showing that the Earth Movement enjoyed the support of several other bands and numerous artistic groups. It was Achilles' view, which he shared with the negotiators, that an increasing number of people were gravitating towards an idea of climate change that was nourished by negative, at times even threatening, tones against the human part of the universe. While Achilles and the negotiators were discussing the matter, Angelo informed them that the Nordic Alliance had put out a press release announcing rewards to anyone with information about the Svalbard seeds and a major reward to those returning the seeds. The negotiators condemned the decision particularly for the risk it would pose to all parties involved.

On the following day Annabelle was going to leave for the Sahara Desert, so a lunch had been organised to wish her well in her first mission outside the office. Romeo had prepared some tasty food and organised 'the best weekly dish' competition. Negotiators and rhetoricians joined in and the gathering was marked by a family-like atmosphere. Romeo had also prepared a cake in the form and colour of the Sahara Desert that put the whole office in an ecstatic mood. Later, Achilles went over to Annabelle's office to discuss some last details before her departure. He mentioned Claire and John, who were also going to attend the conference, adding that she should keep them in mind in case of an emergency. Some other scientists came in to say goodbye. Martha and George gave her a little flacon that she at first mistook for one of René

114

Lalique's elegant creations, which Annabelle was familiar with because her mother collected them. In quickly recollecting herself, though, she noticed that it was a small scientific jar. The flacon had three separate compartments in which it was possible to store different samples. In taking leave from Annabelle, Martha gave her some advice.

"Pay attention to everything; don't dismiss what is unknown to you."

Soon after, Lucillo and Parys took her to JFK Airport for her first solo assignment as a GAIC's representative.

Achilles had often thought about Åke, not knowing exactly how to interpret his silence. He had not heard from him since their mission to the Svalbard vault. He was, therefore, pleased when Åke got in touch with him that afternoon. He was in New York and proposed to pay Achilles a visit. An hour later, they were chatting amicably. Before getting down to work, though, Achilles took Åke on an office tour and introduced him to the GAIC staff. The last station of the office tour was the café where they met Romeo, who welcomed Åke with his unaffected style.

When they finally sat down in Achilles' office, Åke told him that he had been busy with building a miniaturised model of the internal rooms of the Svalbard vault. This had helped him, he said, to see some details he had overlooked during his two visits to the vault. But he was clearly disappointed at his inability to pick up more unusuality. In response, Achilles observed that perhaps there was not much unusuality in the theft. Åke politely rejected Achilles' suggestion by observing that perhaps this was a new type of unusuality; one that required a mental leap that he had unfortunately not been able to make yet.

"Something very strange is going on," Åke said, "and yet I cannot totally understand what it is."

"Is not the theft of the seed a past event?" Achilles asked.

"For some reason, I believe that the theft is still going on," responded Åke, "but I cannot explain the particulars."

"But what makes you think that the theft is still going on?"

"As mentioned before, I have reconstructed the whole place in my miniature and I sense that the doors are the issue here but listen to this, I believe that on the day the seeds were stolen, there were two groups of thieves in the vault. If you look at the situation attentively, you'll notice that only the basic seeds were stolen while the seeds stored in the other rooms were neglected. This makes me think that the thieves must have been interrupted by something or somebody and as a result, they did not take more seeds and went straight to the most important ones, leaving in a hurry and more importantly, carrying the seeds in their bags rather than using a trolley. In fact, I noticed an abandoned trolley behind the door of one of the storage rooms. I have reasons to believe that it was the thieves who blew up the main entrance to the vault."

"Interesting!"

"Thus," continued Åke with vigour, "I believe that somebody else must have gone into the vault on the same day as the thieves who were after the seeds. The choice of the same day might have been by chance or design. But I assure you that to enter the vault via the ropes or even via the waterhole is professional work that must have required extraordinary equipment and skills, so let's call those who used the ropes, the professional thieves. In my view, it was the professionals who overturned the shelves and they did so because they were not interested in the seeds but in something else, something that I believe is stored behind a hidden door."

Åke's piercing eyes rested on Achilles' face who noticed how the sun rays coming through the window made Åke's gaze shine.

"So the seeds are only one of two problems?"

"We need to break through the hidden door!" cried Åke.

Achilles admired Åke's sharp analysis, particularly because he had never mentioned to him the possibility that there was a fifth door.

"You seem to be very sure that there is a fifth hidden door," Achilles observed, "but you cannot prove it, can you?"

"Unfortunately, there is no certainty here," replied Åke. He was quick to add, though, that this time certainty was not needed. "You see," continued Åke, "the fact is that the second and third doors have the same length and width as the first and fourth doors, although only two-thirds of their door panels open. The same construction material was used for all of the storage rooms, as confirmed by Roman. However, and it's a big however, when I examined the floor in the storage rooms, I noticed a slightly changed colour in the area that I would roughly locate in proximity to doors two and three. A normal or untrained eye could not have easily detected such change."

Achilles made a mental note about the last bit since it was not clear to him whether Åke was revealing something about himself that he had overlooked.

"I touched the floor and it felt cold and wet," said Åke, speaking almost mechanically as if he was following some distant thoughts. Then, remembering that Achilles was looking at him, he regained his presence and touched his forehead. "Of course," he then cried out, "the storage room behind the hidden door must lie deeper into the soil or even be under the water level to cause the ground to be wet. Of course, they could not put the seeds there since they would have simply rotted."

"Considering the cold temperature and the icy water, nothing could be stored in that room, isn't it?" Achilles asked.

"Only one thing that is not a polar animal could withstand that icy cold," said Åke smiling.

"Water?" asked Achilles.

"Exactly!" echoed Åke.

"But why on earth would one put water in water?"

"Good question," replied Åke.

"Perhaps, it's a special kind of water…" Achilles mused as if speaking to himself.

"Or new water?" saying which Åke rose and moved towards the door. "Have to leave you now. Will get back in touch." He was gone in a flash. Again, Achilles was taken aback by the speed of Åke's movements.

Thinking about the events of the recent weeks, Achilles was now wondering what might happen next. He was now facing two issues, neither of which was close to resolution. *I need an icebreaker!*

Chapter 16

A turn of events brought some respite. Reverber's initiative to offer a reward to anyone who brought back the stolen seeds backfired. The website of the Nordic Alliance was flooded with messages by people who claimed to have information about the seeds. More troublesome were stories about groups of people of dubious background who had infiltrated the scene close to the band *Save the Earth*. These people promised money to anyone who could provide information about the leaders of the Earth Movement. One day, the front singer of the music band narrowly escaped a kidnapping attempt. Several prominent members of the movement now realised that they might be at risk of being harmed by people who wanted the big rewards promised by the Nordic Alliance. There seemed to be a general assumption that the movement was involved in the theft of the seeds, and that assumption made the movement leaders understand that the Nordic Alliance's money could become their death sentence. After long discussions and painful admissions, the movement leaders made contact with Achilles' office. They spoke with Angelo and requested a meeting with Achilles or his representatives to discuss their situation. Achilles asked the head negotiator to organise a meeting between two members of his senior staff and the movement's representatives. He urged them to find a consensual solution for the return of the seeds. The two negotiators informed Achilles that the members of the movement admitted having stolen the seeds and were prepared to let Achilles know their whereabouts in exchange for protection.

Achilles met with the head negotiator and his senior aides to discuss the matter and discovered that they were disinclined to accept the movement's conditions for the return of the seeds. It was a general understanding that ONO could not be blackmailed and therefore the transaction suggested by the movement – seeds against protection – could not be accepted. The negotiators, however, saw room for further talks with the movement. They met again with its members and urged them to return the seeds unconditionally, for only then could the negotiators listen to their grievances. The head negotiator and his deputies were also inclined to invite the movement's representatives, along with the music band, to the global negotiation that Achilles was planning. Their participation, they said, would give the youth the opportunity to explain their action and take responsibility for the theft of the seeds from the vault of Svalbard. Achilles was pleased with the suggestion which showed a convergence of opinions on this matter. Negotiators and rhetoricians were now slowly starting to gear up for the upcoming global negotiation which became immediately known as the 'Humanity versus Climate Change Negotiation.'

In the meantime, anger was mounting against the Nordic Alliance. To protect itself, the board of the alliance decided to recall the rewards and remove Reverb from his position as director. The decision to recall the rewards was met with anger in some quarters and threats were made against the members of the board and especially Reverb. In the end, the alliance had suffered a blow to its reputation because the rewards clearly showed a lack of wisdom. Hence, the Nordic Alliance too was invited to take part in the planned global negotiation, where it would be given the opportunity to explain itself in terms of its values and its future plans with regard to the collection and storage of new seeds.

Preparations for the global negotiation were now underway across all agencies that assisted GAIC. Soon invitations would start to go out and reach all corners of the world. Achilles wrote to the powerful Industrial Business Economic Financial Representation (IBEFR) asking for a meeting with their leaders. His request was immediately granted. It was not an everyday occurrence to have Achilles visit them in their palace. When he arrived, the entire innovation nobility was waiting for him. No one would have missed the opportunity to experience first-hand what it meant to deal with ONO and its top negotiator. When Achilles entered the room where the entrepreneurs were awaiting him, he was stunned by the luxury and pomp. He soon noticed though that money rather than elegance was displayed. Tension was palpable but Achilles' charm soon softened the general feelings and as a result, he was given the place of honour.

"The reason I'm here," he stated, "is to invite reflection from your quarters on some events that are creating a sense of confusion in our young, splitting the scientific community, and people in general. It is a confusion that is increasingly expressed through misanthropic views, which are particularly upsetting to those who believe in humanity." His warm voice filled the whole room. He knew that he was using language that was detested in the palace but the people in attendance would never show their dislike openly to him. Addiction to innovation had not gone so far as to kill off decorum.

"Therefore," Achilles continued, "ONO is inviting you to respond to the worries and fears of many people and to help us find a consensual solution." Achilles spoke gently, asking for their cooperation. They appreciated his speech but were also aware that he had the power to force a negotiation on them should they reject his offer. Mindful of this, the IBEFR's vice-president used moderate language in his reply.

"We are not sure how we can deal with those confused youths, scientists and people; they seem to lack imagination."

"Imagination needs courage to manifest itself. Courage is a virtue that must be cultivated," Achilles observed. "Sometimes the conditions necessary for such a virtue to emerge must be created consensually."

"We are self-made people," the president said, "we don't understand this population living in perpetual fears and need of nannies."

Achilles said nothing at first. He thought that in order to get the goodwill of the Representation, he needed to make them consent to the negotiation freely.

"I have always thought," he said warmly, "that the power of truly self-made people lies in their ability to see opportunities where others only see fears, threats, and obstacles."

Many smiled at such a move that looked like an elegant checkmate. Some applauded, perhaps the more sensible among the self-made, until the IBEFR president, in rising from his throne joined in the applause and promised that the

Representation would attend the negotiation in good faith. Everybody stood up and hands were shaken. Achilles showed his appreciation and spent a good hour with them, inquiring about developments and plans. They happily answered his questions and gave him information. He caught them by surprise, however, by suddenly turning the conversation towards water and asking them about their views on this topic. They had expected Achilles to speak about the risks of new industrial and technological developments but water truly put them into a spin.

"We will carry out more research on water and let you know our position," the president said hesitantly. He did not know whether Achilles had inadvertently or intentionally revealed to him something important. The president, however, knew one thing for sure, namely that whatever Achilles spoke about deserved full attention. Immediately after this exchange, Achilles thanked them and left.

No sooner had Achilles vacated the palace of the Representation than the president sent a message to all of his closest aides. He ordered them to establish a taskforce on water at once. He named Margareta Bell and Leo van den Horst, two of the best members of the management group, as the chairs of the new taskforce. The president wanted a full report about all aspects of water by the end of the week. "Spare no money."

While, on his way home, Achilles was reviewing his meeting with the Representation he realised how the negotiation he had in mind was growing in importance. He felt that the negotiation resulted not only from a wish to find common ground between different visions of the future but that it also stemmed from an existential necessity. New and old problems needed sorting, new plans were wanted and above all, informed consent had to be secured and implemented. And the support of all good governments guaranteed. Notified of the upcoming negotiation, governments had already confirmed their attendance.

Chapter 17

Annabelle looked out of the window and saw the Blue City, the capital of the Tuareg confederation. The plane touched down at nine in the morning. As soon as she reached the airport hall, somebody holding a sign of the University of the Desert approached her. Annabelle was not the only person to be met in the airport hall for, soon after her arrival, five other people joined her and the person holding the sign. The travellers were taken to a smaller room where other people, who had probably arrived earlier, were already waiting. Twenty people altogether. The man who had met them in the hall checked their names and identities with marvellous efficiency. Annabelle noticed that her conference tag contained her name and the name of her university. There was no mention of the acronym GAIC on the badge, which pleased her, for that would shield her from being the target of questions about Achilles. The delegates were transferred to a bus terminal and then taken to the University of the Desert, which was located in close proximity to the Sahara Desert. From there, they continued to a nearby hotel for room allocation. The conference was to start in an hour with a welcome buffet followed by the presentations of the keynote speakers. In addition to Annabelle, there were five other PhD students attending the conference.

She looked around and immediately recognised Claire and John for Achilles had shown her a photograph of his two friends. They were busy talking to some other delegates. She observed their body language and the people they were talking with. But Annabelle soon realised that she too had become an object of observation. Annabelle noticed two distinguished people looking at her across the hall. They smiled at her when their eyes met and Annabelle smiled back. Elegance was a natural, and salient, feature of Annabelle's personality, for wherever she went, she met admirers. It was obvious to everyone attending the event that she was the youngest among the attendees but people also noticed that she was the most gracious too.

Everybody went to their rooms to refresh from the trip; without any doubt, the rooms were fabulous. The windows looked out over a sea of sand that was undulated by the vivid dunes, an image that made her feel dreamy. Annabelle felt all the beauty of this image and she could have stayed in her room for another little while to admire the soft sand if her sense of duty had not awakened her to the need to join the conference gathering. On entering the room, Annabelle noticed that some delegates were already sitting at the dining tables while others were still standing; they had formed small groups and were engaged in animated conversations. She was looking for a table when she was addressed by the two people she had noticed observing her earlier. They introduced themselves: Gwafa Illi Tin Hinan princess of the Blue People and owner of the university and Amastan Badis Hammadit, husband of the princess and rector of the university. Annabelle felt embarrassed for their singling her out but they quickly made her feel at ease by enquiring if the room was to her satisfaction to which Annabelle replied that her room was simply fabulous. They seemed to appreciate her commendation, and after some small talk their conversation turned to Achilles. He had explicitly asked Annabelle to convey his best wishes to the princess and her husband and to mention his intention to visit their wonderful city as soon as feasible. She dutifully repeated Achilles' words and found them very pleased with the message.

"There is no other person in the world," the princess replied, "whom we would like to welcome with more pleasure to our desert than Achilles." Annabelle thanked them. Hereafter, they wished her a productive time at the conference and exhorted her to take the trip to the dunes planned for the coming Sunday, which was to be the last day of the conference. Annabelle assured them that she would certainly not miss the opportunity.

She moved towards the dining tables but not before taking a closer look at the buffet; it filled the ambience with aromatic scents and fabulous colours through the richness of all the fruits and tastes of the Sahara regions. When she finally sat down, she discovered that her table companions were relaxed and making conversation in a respectful way.

After lunch, Amastan Badis declared the conference officially open. In his welcome address, he talked about a new era for the desert and its inhabitants and afterwards introduced the keynote speakers. The first was a professor of desert architecture and in her talk, she carefully explained how during the last fifty years the desert had shifted through the formation of faults that made some parts of the desert dangerous even for experienced travellers. One of these faults, she added, was located in a central area of the desert to which the upcoming Sunday's trip would take the delegates. The professor further said that scientists had been wondering for quite some time now why those faults had appeared and if there was an empty space beneath them or a submerged ancient city or perhaps other important things such as water, oil, precious stones, or minerals. It was one of the goals of the organisers of the conference, the speaker concluded, to find out whether the movement of the desert was a sign of promising developments or just changes in the sand mass.

The next keynote speech was delivered by two members of a scientific consortium who had been studying the effects of climate change on deserts for many years. The content of their talk was vastly different from the one that the delegates had just listened to. These speakers took a critical view on the faults, which in their views were a direct result of climate change, and observed that the formation of new abysses and canyons beneath the desert was the effect of sand being sucked down deep into the earth. The speakers predicted that climate change would make vast areas of the desert unsafe and that local earthquakes would put at risk the regions bordering on the sand. In concluding their talk, the speakers warned against false positives, particularly when it came to the luxurious vegetation that had followed the generous rains of the recent years because that rain was itself an effect of climate change. "Don't be fooled," they cried, "climate change is not a positive force!"

The discussion that followed the two presentations was dominated by a group of scientists which also included Claire and John. These scientists were less pessimistic than the previous two speakers and admitted the possibility that there might be life beneath the desert surface. John went so far as to state that it might be life of a kind never seen before. John's statement impressed Annabelle as well as the other delegates, some of whom asked further questions. In his answers, though, John tried to be more cautious than he had been in his previous statement and warned that until compelling evidence was produced through new excavations, his conclusions should be taken as an optimistic view on the events now taking place deep in the desert.

The conference continued until Saturday and the conference delegates enjoyed it thoroughly. Annabelle understood all the importance of what was going on at the meeting and at the end of each conference day sent short reports to Achilles, Angelo, George, and Martha, as well as to Lucillo and Parys. It was Achilles' view that people working in teams should share as many insights as possible. Back in New York, Annabelle's colleagues were keen to read her reports and could hardly wait to have her back and hear first-hand about the desert faults.

Sunday finally arrived and the delegates were flown in a propeller plane to a small hangar situated in an area of the desert that was usually inaccessible to travellers. The conference organisers had erected a tent near the hangar and on their arrival, the visitors were offered tea and dates. The grunting of camels waiting with their shepherds outside the tent signalled to the delegates that the last stretch of their trip would be on the back of camels. It took two hours to reach the areas where the first excavations had been carried out, and from there, another half an hour to the place where the new faults had appeared. Annabelle immediately realised that she would not have noticed the most recent fault if it had not been for the two slim and high stones that pierced the sand and stretched toward the sky, a phenomenon never seen before in the Sahara. The Tuaregs had constructed bridges around the fault to help experts examine the depth of the sand canyons, as archaeologists described them. Everybody walked carefully on the bridges, the last of which allowed the visitors to move close to the two high stones.

When Annabelle and three other people were standing near the two stones, unexpectedly and abruptly, the sand caved in, threatening to drag them down into the canyon. Annabelle's reflexes made her instinctively stretch out her hands and was surprised to find something to hold onto. She pulled herself up to a flat area, which stood higher up and looked safe. The other three visitors were less quick in their reaction and were now standing on a clearing that seemed about to give in at any moment. While she was holding onto that something, Annabelle realised that she was actually standing on a hard surface. She pushed down with her feet and was pleased, although astonished, to find that it was a stone. On pressing down again, she found that it was steady. She then realised that she was holding onto a wooden rafter, probably lost or forgotten by those who had built the bridges. She felt thankful to the bridge workers for that piece of wood that was once irremediably lost in sand and was now invested with a new function by new circumstances. She closed her hands tight around the drafter while considering what to do next, particularly if help was going to be delayed. She turned her head to the left to see if there was a sand terrace to which she could climb up to safety, and indeed, she noticed one not far from where she stood. She immediately realised though that to reach it she would need to swing her body by first pressing down hard on the stone with her feet and then by jumping up to the higher terrace. *Will the stone beneath my feet remain steady if I push down hard on it?* Panic-stricken, she was considering her chances of success, when she suddenly noticed a little plant that seemed to be growing out of the wooden rafter. The plant's leaves were dotted with water drops. They reminded her of the droplets of the early dew when it softly covers mountain flowers. Looking more closely, Annabelle noticed that the little plant was lying in a small pond of luminous water. She was exceedingly stunned at this discovery since no water was supposed to withstand the heat of the desert.

She pressed one more time against the stone under her feet, and in discovering that the stone was still steady, she slowly loosened her left hand, while holding onto the drafter with her right hand, and grabbed the little flacon that Martha had given her. She kept it in a small leather bag that she had fastened around her upper right arm. Moving her left hand carefully, she grabbed the flacon and pressed with her thumb on the lid of the first section, which opened unexpectedly quickly. She immersed the flacon in the pond to let the water and the small plant, which was gently floating on it, slowly slide into the flacon. She then pressed down the lid with her thumb, a firm click confirmed that it was now hermetically closed. Immediately thereafter, she saw more of the same luminous water lying in a larger wood interstice. She opened the lid of the second section of her glass flacon, again by pressing on it with her thumb and filled it with the water. She took all the liquid she could. She then pushed down the lid and a firm click confirmed that also this section was now closed hermetically. Before leaving for the faults, Annabelle had put a small spoon in her leather bag to collect sand samples. Faithful to her original intention, she now set the flacon in the sand, pressed on the lid of the third section and filled it with sand. After closing the lid, she carefully returned the flacon and spoon back into the pocket of her leather bag.

The collection of the three samples had made her forget for a while her own situation, at length, however, she recollected where she was. The idea of moving up to the next sand terrace that she had considered before finding the plant and the water, did not appeal to her anymore for she now realised that it had been dictated by panic. She concluded that it was safer for her to stay where she was and wait quietly for her rescuers and when they arrived, she was easily lifted to safety. After some time, the other three members of the excursion were also saved. Annabelle replied graciously to the friendly inquiries of the other delegates about her well-being. The incident was clear evidence to the conference delegates that the desert was moving in unexpected ways and that it was a matter of urgency to find out why.

The group returned to the Blue City and then to the hotel in order to prepare for dinner. Once in her room, Annabelle took out her flacon and noticed with amazement that neither the droplets on the leaves of the small plant nor the water had disappeared. She wondered about the nature of her finding and found the content of her flacon mysterious. She hoped to have its mystery explained by the GAIC scientists. She resolved to put the flacon in her necessaire bag, among her perfumes and creams. She then took a refreshing shower and after adjusting her hair, she put on a dark blue dress. It was a present from a friend of hers, a fashion designer who had made it on the occasion of Annabelle's trip to the desert. It was long and slightly décolleté, falling nicely around her shoulders. The dress was made of raw silk, with generous sleeves made of light satin. The sleeves were open at the back exposing her elbows every time she moved her arms and each sleeve was fastened at the wrist with a white pearl. The large and slightly transparent gown fell elegantly on her legs and its light fabric softly enveloped them at every step. In contrast to the shades of her dress, Annabelle's hair had the colour of the Sahara sand when it is touched by the sun; it was naturally wavy and moved softly on her back.

Her recent experience in the desert, yes, the danger she had faced, conferred an air of maturity on her that invited admiration. And when she entered the great reception room, Annabelle was courted by everyone. Had she been less desperate to return to her room, she would have enjoyed the conversations and flirts a bit more. While she was experiencing a mixture of tension and joy, Annabelle was addressed by the princess and her husband. They both admired her dress and expressed great appreciation for her presence. "We hope to see you back again soon," said the princess with a smile. Wrapped in soft elegant fabric and wearing splendid jewels, they both looked enigmatic. Annabelle felt overcome by their generosity and suddenly felt guilty for what she was hiding from them. She lowered her eyes and tried to say something that matched her hosts' address but her mind, which was usually quick, now deserted her. Amastan Badis and the princess Gwafa Illi were sensible people and in noticing her embarrassment, which they judged was caused by her age, stretched out their hands and wished her a safe trip home but not without observing that the desert

133

was a place where people could have the most extraordinary encounters. What at first sounded like an innocuous observation, on reflection appeared to her like a hidden message.

The next day, she was to fly back to New York. She decided to keep the flacon in her personal necessaire bag since it looked like a perfume bottle. On the following morning, all of the conference delegates were collected at four o'clock and taken to the Blue City airport from where they flew to their different destinations.

She arrived in New York on Monday afternoon and was picked up at the airport by Lucillo and Parys. When she saw them, tears of joy ran down her cheek. They spent the evening together; she recounted her trip to the desert describing minutely what she had found there. After wondering if this could be something of importance, they concluded that perhaps she should share her story with Achilles before making it public. Annabelle made contact with him, who was delighted to hear that she had returned home safely. Before he could further enquire about her trip, Annabelle, unable to hold back, started to speak about her stay in the Blue City. She hastily came to the main point and described what had happened in the desert and the samples she had collected. She also related the two conversations she had had with princess Gwafa Illi and her husband. They had expressed their hopes to see Achilles in the Blue City, and they had reminded her that the desert is full of unexpected encounters. Annabelle also informed Achilles that his friends Claire and John had worked very closely with the organisers of the conference, often sitting in deep conversation with Amastan Badis.

Achilles listened with great interest and based on what Annabelle was telling him, he instinctively sensed that the events that she was describing, particularly what she had found in the desert, were in some ways linked to what was happening in Svalbard. Acknowledging the importance of his own conclusion, despite having to admit to himself that he had no solid evidence to prove what he was conjecturing, he judged it prudent to let an ONO bodyguard collect her from home the following morning.

During the past few days, Achilles had identified a few logical patterns in the events that had taken place in the vault of Svalbard. They increasingly appeared less like the product of coincidences and more like the acts of a script that somebody had written and was now playing in front of his eyes. He only wished to know the whole script. He thought that it was a matter of paramount importance from now on to move with care and plan every step to avoid being at the mercy of an invisible mastermind. He needed to anticipate at least some of the events that were in that script. The vault of Svalbard was now casting a longer shadow than he had ever imagined.

Chapter 18

After his conversation with Annabelle, Achilles called a morning meeting for the following day, Tuesday, to which he invited his scientific assistants, senior aides, and junior secretaries. He called an afternoon meeting with the negotiators and a final meeting with the rhetoricians for the day after. On noticing that the invitation to the meetings came from Achilles himself, everybody concluded that they were emergency calls. No one knew by then, not even Achilles, that the following day would mark a historical leap ahead for life on the planet earth. Achilles also invited Professor Albert Melitus from New York to join their morning session at ten o'clock. The professor was an expert on water. Although Achilles was still struggling with connecting all the bits lying in front of him, he had understood that water was the issue at stake and that the mystery of the hidden door in the vault of Svalbard had something to do with water.

On Tuesday, Achilles went to work at six in the morning and noticed with great delight that Romeo had prepared a breakfast buffet for the whole office. On being told that important meetings were planned for the day, he had decided to prepare some extra food for the morning meal. The smell of croissants and chocolate, cheese and ham pies, apple torte and cinnamon biscuits, tea, espresso, cappuccino, hot chocolate and all that Romeo and his assistants had put out on the buffet, would have lifted the spirits of the most afflicted person. As Achilles sat down for breakfast, Romeo joined him and updated him about the champion leagues, new surfing competitions, baseball encounters, fencing championships and so forth. They never spoke about office matters unless Achilles brought them up.

"Anything new from the hospitality scene?"

"Lots of new people in town, my friends tell me."

"Unusual for the time?"

"Unusual and strange."

"Any theory why that's so?"

"People say that conferences about water are succeeding one another and investors are filling the hotels, particularly in the financial district," Romeo said.

"Hm. Keep me informed about any news you get about those people, will you?"

"Certainly."

While they were talking, the junior secretaries came in speaking fast and loud. They went up to Achilles to say hello, and Annabelle took the opportunity to give him her leather bag containing the glass flacon. Afterwards the three juniors went over to the buffet, admiring it and joking with Romeo who welcomed everybody with his reassuring presence. Later, Achilles took the flacon to Martha and George, who were waiting for him in the ONO's main scientific laboratory; he asked them to prepare for the arrival of a visitor who would carry out tests on the samples collected by Annabelle.

The night before Achilles had sent a message to Angelo asking him to dig deep in the former NU archives to find out if the Tuareg people had ever applied for world heritage protection of the areas comprising the territories of their Confederation, namely their desert. When Angelo came to the breakfast room he immediately went up to Achilles, who was quickly checking the news, and informed him that he had found an old application from the 1950s, filed by Aderfi Tamari Amanar, the grandfather of the present princess Gwafa Illi. He had submitted it in the name of his wife the Queen Dihya Safiyya Tin Hanan who had requested that the desert, where the Tuaregs had lived for centuries, be put under World Heritage protection. That request was made public by the former NU and none of Tuaregs' powerful neighbours ever challenged it. The lack of challenge was an important precondition for the award of special status to designated areas since NU would not have overlooked opposition from third parties before granting protection to a geographical site. Strangely, NU had subsequently failed to progress the application of the Tuaregs. Because ONO had retained unchanged most of the rules of NU with regard to World Heritage protection of cultural and natural environments, the lack of opposition to the application filed by the Tuaregs now made it possible to process it and get it through. Achilles was acting quickly, and for a second he wondered if he was not perhaps too precipitous in reviving such an old application. He also feared that processing the application of the Tuaregs could attract opposition from multinationals and western countries that in the past had insisted on keeping the Sahara an off-limit zone. Achilles still did not see a direct link between the polar north and the desert south but something inside him was telling him to waste no time. Trusting his instinct, he asked Angelo to complete the application and add it to the other four applications already with the ONO World Heritage Committee, which was expected to make a decision about them today.

Achilles went back to his office and contacted the head of the committee and its members by a video call. He told them that he was about to file a new application, which he explained to them in details. Before ending the video call he invited them to consider the application of the Tuaregs with the utmost urgency since, he added, it had been overlooked for decades. Afterwards, he prepared for the upcoming morning meeting. Despite the tension that his decision to promote the application of the Tuaregs might cause, he felt confident that it was the right move to make. Angelo finalised the Tuareg application in a flash and went to the office of the director-general to collect his signature. On noticing that Achilles had already signed the application, the director-general did not hesitate to approve it. For some reason, Achilles' sense of urgency had a contagious effect. Angelo then sent the application to the World Heritage Committee for approval. By six o'clock in the afternoon five new areas were put under ONO's protection. These areas included a deep region of the Amazon Forest, a sacred place in an Aboriginal community in Central Australia, a recently discovered Jakarta temple to the goddess of beauty, an ancient city in Azerbaijan, and the desert of the Tuaregs. ONO's heritage protection was far more effective than the protection that NU gave in the past and took any attempts to undermine its tutelage very seriously and always acted against them with decisiveness.

Achilles opened the morning meeting at nine o'clock, which the director-general also attended, by recapitulating the events that had occurred since the theft of the seeds in the

Svalbard vault. He then asked Annabelle to summarise her trip to the conference and speak about her finding. Once Annabelle had concluded her report, Achilles shared his view about the vault of Svalbard. He stated that he had good reasons to believe that the hidden chamber in the vault of Svalbard might contain a secret. He then informed his people that Professor Melitus would address the meeting after completing some tests in Martha and George's laboratory. The professor was shown Annabelle's plant covered with the water droplets and the water pond in which it was lying, he was not told though where they came from. Melitus was asked to analyse the water and at the conclusion of his tests, to prepare a report which would be regarded as classified information. As soon as Martha informed Achilles that the professor and his assistants were ready to share their findings, Achilles invited them to address the meeting via a video call from the laboratory. Melitus began to speak hastily and summarised his assessment.

"We have carried out several tests," Melitus stated, "and they all seem to point to one conclusion." His look was bright, the face slightly coloured. He seemed barely able to contain his excitement. "If we are correct in our estimations and results, which we have arrived at after numerous tests, what we have here is a kind of new water, something a thousand times more precious than usual water. It does not evaporate and it does not absorb bacteria. The mice we have given it to have shown no need for water, even after forcing salt into their bodies. This means that people who drink this water might not need to quench their thirst again for many years, perhaps never again, because it remains in the body and maintains all the bodily fluids in balance over very long stretches." Silence followed Professor Melitus' speech, and it lasted for several minutes.

"If we are correct," Melitus resumed talking, "this water could revolutionise everything. Now unimaginable products could be created, many of the illnesses still plaguing humans and animals could be defeated. In fact, I believe that this new water has also curative effects, that it may give longevity but this," Melitus added in a more cautionary tone, "I would have to examine further in conjunction with medical researchers."

The information imparted by professor Melitus had a major impact on everybody.

"What does this water mean in terms of future life on the planet earth?" Achilles asked.

"It means that we are dealing with a sort of water that neither evaporates nor freezes. It remains a lively liquid all the time. This water," continued Melitus in a solemn tone, "is far, far more precious than all the oil, metals and gold together currently hidden in earth." He paused briefly and then added with vigour that such water could unleash a furious war since everybody would try to get it.

These words made Annabelle tremble and deeply impressed all the others.

The director-general now wondered why Achilles had put the desert of the Tuaregs on the Heritage protection list in response to an application that was filed such a long time ago and if that decision was connected to the new water. Should any connection exist, no matter how small, he reasoned, then Achilles had shown superior intelligence. *He is always one step ahead of everybody!*

Their eyes met, Achilles smiled at him, and the director-general immediately understood that ONO was now perhaps protecting more than a piece of desert. Worries instantly clouded his mind. He sensed that Achilles could become an even more wanted target of the enemies of GAIC and specially informed consent.

Chapter 19

Melitus and his colleagues left the building soon after delivering their report. Achilles resumed the proceedings and asked for an update from those who had been assigned tasks at the previous meeting. Lucillo was to start. He had shifted through all public research on glaciers and permafrost and found that many scientists working in the field considered the mix of icy water and glaciers to be very corrosive. Some other scientists believed that the oldest glaciers and permafrost dated back one-and-a-half to two million years and that the soil on which they had expanded so mighty might be contaminated with carbon dioxin gases and ancient viruses as well as bacteria. The latter could infect the earth and life in general should they be released into the environment through the melting of the ice. Lucillo continued his report by stating that according to all scientists, the infections that ancient agents could cause included anthrax, smallpox, botulism, and bubonic plague plus all sorts of fungi and infections probably unknown to today's medicine and against which no immunity was yet known. And this was the reason why, he concluded, bacteria and viruses now figured high on the list of predictable and unpredictable risks. Lucillo was listened to with a certain degree of anxiety.

Achilles asked him if any of the scientists had advanced bold theses about the glaciers and the effects of their melting. In response Lucillo mentioned a recent article by John Delafort, a name familiar to Achilles since he was Claire's husband. Delafort believed that there was safer drinkable water in the desert than at the North Pole. Lucillo said that Delafort had been criticised for this suggestion and that his thesis seemed to represent a minority position within the scientific community. Achilles listened with great attention and so did Annabelle who had met John at the conference.

It was now Parys's turn to summarise his activities. He had just returned from a visit to his Detroit man, the collector of natural artefacts. The collector had told Parys that as a young scientist he had spent lots of time conducting research at the North Pole and that he, therefore, knew the ground around the Svalbard vault quite well. He confided to Parys that there were safe caves in the area and that many years ago he had left some marine samples in a secret cave but never returned to collect them. He added that it was not easy to access that cave in winter for its entrance was covered by a thick block of ice that extended down from a terrace and semi-covered the passage into the cave; but in summer the area in the front of the cave turned into a pond surrounded by some thin grass. Mr. Detroit, as Parys referred to him, sometimes lost his lucidity, particularly when he spoke about the past and when he did so his face turned sad. He would quickly regain composure though and talk about his natural library. Parys mentioned the Earth Movement and his collector gave him to understand that he knew the movement and some of its people; they were not on good terms, the collector said to Parys, because he had refused to store something for them.

Parys had pressed him to reveal the nature of their dispute but Mr. Detroit had dodged the question preferring to speak about other things such as the secrets of the oceans and the dangers of the glaciers for water and people. Suddenly, his collector was tired and started repeating himself. His last words were, "My dear friend, life is hidden in the least obvious places," and after uttering them he went to a bed that stood in a corner of his large room and fell asleep.

Meher had returned from India where she had failed to find more information about genetically manipulated bacteria. She had therefore little to report. Somebody, however, had sent her the link to that mysterious Instant Sensory platform that had published the article about the three bacteria experiments and with some luck, she said, was hoping to retrieve it.

Adam had been at Mount View University where he took an advanced course in complex algorithms, the new science of problem-solving through mathematical thinking and machine learning. He again explained the nature of complex algorithms, CAs as he preferred to call them, which could be benevolent when designed to protect human life or malevolent when designed to conquer ruthlessly. This latter expression deeply impressed Achilles since 'to conquer' was a verb that had lost all its appeal in everyday parlance. Adam said that CAs' power seemed infinite and so was the amount of effort that experts had to make to understand them. He observed that the creation of a truly complex algorithm seemed to *him* an almost impossible task for a single human mind. Some of his former colleagues, however, believed that two complex algorithms had been created a few decades ago, and that judging from traces left behind by their applications and movements in some supercomputers, they were still active. Not only his colleagues at Mount View University but also those from the Massachusetts Institute of A.I. believed that the two algorithms, and perhaps some others created later, had become almost independent through machine learning and that they were now too sophisticated even for today's supercomputers, meaning that to control such algorithms quantum computers would be required. A short pause followed Adam's speech which was broken by him.

"How much time do I have to crack the algorithm that controls the hidden door in the vault of Svalbard?" he asked Achilles.

"One day," Achilles replied. He then informed them that he had asked Colonel Olsen to organise a new mission to the Svalbard vault and that his goal was to enter the hidden chamber. He added that Martha, George, and Roman were going to Svalbard in a few hours to prepare the operation from the ONO side and that Olsen had agreed to let them stay at the Longyearbyen military base. A second team would fly to the base on the following day, Wednesday. The mission to the vault would take place on Thursday. Here turning to the director-general, Achilles asked him how long he could keep governments and their agencies calm.

"As long as you need me to," answered the director. The reason for this latter exchange between Achilles and the director-general was that governments were pressuring for more clarity about the theft of the seeds and also about any other issues that were still unresolved. A pause followed, during which everybody felt a strong sense of determination. At length, Achilles resumed talking.

"Meher, with the help of the interns and the support of the other members of the office, will watch over the laboratories, including the one where professor Melitus had carried out his tests. Annabelle, Lucillo, and Parys will deal with the media and provide their representatives with information about unclassified material." Achilles asked everybody in his office, rhetoricians and negotiators included, to be extra vigilant until further instructions. The director-general took the opportunity to let everybody know that he had already doubled the number of guards outside and inside the ONO building. On his way out of the meeting, Achilles went to Romeo.

"I'm leaving on Wednesday. Keep your eyes wide open and also look after the juniors."

As he was leaving the café, Achilles saw Annabelle walk up the corridor looking worried. He stopped and waited for her.

"Alright, Annabelle?"

Annabelle gave him a hesitant smile but when she finally spoke, he instantly understood the reason for her hesitancy.

"Should I not tell Gwafa Illi about the plant and the water that I found in their desert?" Her voice was trembling, her eyes filled with apprehension.

A mutual silence took place for some time, during which Achilles' thoughts instantly went through all ONO's priorities and the classified nature of Annabelle's finds. But he soon put an end to all his thinking and warmly said, "Yes, you should."

"When do you suggest I should tell her?"

"Whenever you have an opportunity to talk to her in person."

Annabelle felt relieved. She mentioned that she had not yet sent the princess a thank-you note for her hospitality

147

during the conference but that she was going to do so immediately. "And on this occasion, I'll ask for a private audience with her next time I am in the Blue City."

"Sounds perfect!"

They parted but after a few steps, Achilles stopped and called her back, "Thank you, Annabelle, for being so kind and considerate."

When he finally returned to his room, Achilles called Olsen.

"How well do you know the landscape around the vault?"

"Pretty well," answered the colonel.

"Ever seen a cave with a door made of thick ice and a small front yard which in summer turns into a pond of icy water surrounded by grass?"

Olsen did not reply. "OK. We will try to find it. Any other news?"

"Martha, George, and Roman are going to share more information with you tonight," Achilles replied, "then you'll have to prepare a safety net around Svalbard."

"Hm…" said the colonel, "sounds dramatic."

"Imagine an invasion!" said Achilles to help the colonel understand the possible dangers to his military base and the vault. The colonel immediately saluted Achilles and disappeared from the screen.

While he was sitting on his sofa with his feet up, Achilles received a communication from Colonel James Neill.

"Is it true what we have heard about new water?"

"I have always wondered," replied Achilles, "why Defence never signed our informed consent memorandum of understanding."

"We are ready to do so if this will improve our relations," the colonel replied. Achilles noticed that he was not alone in the room; indeed there were at least five other highly ranked military personnel besides Neill.

"A wise decision," replied Achilles calmly. He wondered if this would not cause some friction with his government but he then concluded that Neill's superiors must have given him permission to go ahead. Achilles excused himself for a minute to give instructions to Angelo regarding the ONO memorandum of understanding to be forwarded to Colonel Neill for signature. Angelo executed the instruction immediately, and in less than ten minutes, Defence was working in partnership with ONO under the civil command of Achilles.

"Replying to your question," Achilles eventually said, "yes, it's probably true."

"What can we do to help?" the military man asked.

"We need to protect a large area in the Sahara desert, near the Blue City, and belonging to the Tuaregs," Achilles replied. He informed Neill and his staff that ONO had granted special status to that part of the desert meaning that it was now under World Heritage protection. He also told him about the faults that had emerged and given rise to speculations about new water sources located under the desert surface. Achilles asked Neill's advice with regard to the enforcement of the protection bestowed by ONO. The military made precise suggestions and afterwards, arrangements were made to initiate cooperation with the people living in that area of the desert. Achilles exhorted Neill to make direct contact with princess Gwafa Illi Tin Hinan to discuss the terms of the ONO protection.

"I think she might need it sooner than she thinks," Achilles said.

"Is all of this related to the theft in the Svalbard vault?" asked the colonel.

"This is something I'm hoping to clarify this week during our next mission to the vault of Svalbard," Achilles answered. Neill replied that he had been informed about the waterhole in the east room of the vault and that he was very concerned about the possibility of foreign forces entering Norway. He asked Achilles for permission to send two of his scientists to join the teams that were going to Svalbard. Achilles agreed to his request, in the firm belief that the more scientists worked for peace, the better. The colonel named two of his scientists and asked his aides to arrange for their immediate transfer from Washington to New York.

Unable to contain his curiosity, the colonel finally asked Achilles to give him a hint about what was at stake in the whole mission.

"Imagine a new global war," replied Achilles. Total silence followed his statement.

"We will move into action swiftly," replied the military man, more accustomed to the language of war than to actions of peace. Neill also offered to take Achilles and his team to the Longyearbyen military base by military plane. The offer was quickly accepted since it was Achilles' view that it was too risky to use commercial flights on this occasion. That this was a wise decision became apparent when on the following day the Norwegian government, on the advice of Olsen, announced a temporary suspension of all commercial and private flights to Svalbard between Wednesday morning and Thursday night due to technical issue at the local airport.

"I sincerely hope," said Achilles to a worried Neill, "that you and one of your deputies will be able to join the ONO team on this highly sensitive mission."

"I'd be honoured to be part of your team," said Neill, saluting Achilles before turning off the communication.

In the evening, Martha, George, and Roman, along with the two Defence scientists, flew to Longyearbyen to meet Olsen. The colonel had already informed the Norwegian government of the upcoming mission and had received full support. Olsen requested a representative of the Norwegian government to attend the mission and the government sent the minister of communication and culture, a young public servant who had distinguished herself in the past for being one of the most informed persons in the country. Finally, on Wednesday morning, Achilles' team also left New York on colonel Neill's military plane.

Chapter 20

On the same day, the director-general of the Organisation Number One published the official list of the five World Heritage sites that had recently been elevated to the status of protected areas. The news caused a great stir in the world, particularly when it came to the areas of the Sahara controlled by the Tuareg Confederation. People wondered why that desert should be given such strong protection, and speculations started to mount about the discovery of new oil or gold under its dunes. The president of IBEFR read the list and jumped out of his chair. *Water, there must be water under that useless sand!* he thought to himself. He immediately called a meeting of the water taskforce and ordered that a team be instantly dispatched to the Blue City and await further instructions. He was not the only one to act. In less than two hours, all flights to the capital were sold out, and the hotels, big and small, filled.

The ONO director-general called the government representatives of the newly protected sites and complimented them on their new status. He also gave them some advice on how to make their nominations work in their countries' favour by applying for supporting funds and cultural initiatives. Finally, he got in contact with Gwafa Illi Tin Hinan. The director-general congratulated her on the nomination and soon exhorted her to initiate activities that would make the desert more accessible to people. The princess thanked him and expressed her delight but then, with natural innocence, wondered why her grandparents' application was overlooked for so long.

"I was a close friend of your grandparents," the director-general replied, "they were persons with great visions, always trying to improve the conditions and fate of their people and both your mother and father indefatigably continued their parent's work."

The princess thanked him, deeply touched by his words.

Gwafa Illi Tin was aware that her grandmother had not studied beyond what was required by her ruling role but her grandfather had a PhD.

"What was grandfather interested in?" She hoped to hear something new from a person so far removed from the family circle.

"Like you," continued the director-general, "your grandfather was a mathematician but he was also a chemist. He saw plenty of possibilities in the desert. Check his archive and you might find the answer you are looking for."

She responded with a slight inclination of the head but said nothing. She still wondered why her grandparents' application had taken so long to get approval if he was such a great friend. On perceiving her doubts, the director-general explained that her grandparents' application was originally submitted to NU but they failed to finalise it. "Achilles recently found it and processed it expeditiously."

"Why?" she asked.

"I believe that his intention was, or I should say: is, to protect you, your children, and your people."

She did not ask for more explanations. She and the director-general continued talking about the various aspects of the nomination and parted on good terms.

After this exchange, Gwafa Illi went to the palace library, where her grandfather's archive was located and sat down at his old desk. Although her grandfather firmly believed in the nomadic principle of living in the desert and accordingly, kept a tent that he used during his long nomadic travels, he had also built a palace and started the first settlement of the Tuaregs that later developed into the Blue City. In the palace, he had his study and the laboratories where he carried out his scientific work. Her father had left her grandfather's apartment and study unchanged, and so had she. Gwafa Illi let her eyes dwell on her grandfather's desk until they rested on an old glass bowl containing a little plant covered with water droplets. The plant was rooted in a sandbank that was itself submerged in water. The bowl was perfectly sealed. She took the ball in her hand and looked at it closely; she now realised that what appeared to be glass was in fact a material she did not recognise. She held up the bowl against the light and studied it for a while then she moved over to the shelves. Grandfather had studied at the best universities of the Sahara region and received scholarships to several western universities and research centres. His shelves, however, did not inspire her. She moved over to her father's shelves at the opposite side of the library and admired how well he had organised his reading material. While she was scrutinising his books, she noticed a notebook squeezed in between two volumes of an old encyclopaedia. She pulled it out and while

154

she was still holding the bowl in her left hand, laid the notebook on a small reading table and quickly went through the pages. She immediately recognised her father's handwriting.

Following the footsteps of grandfather, her father had studied mathematics and chemistry. He too had attended the best universities of the Sahara region and received numerous scholarships to western universities. In his notebook, her father described a method for developing a new type of fine glass by mixing air with silver and water. He explained the chemical compositions necessary to create such fine glass and also included some drawings of glass bowls. In one of his comments, her father said that bowls made of such precious material would be totally sealed and unbreakable, on the margins of his notebook, though, he discussed possible ways by which such bowls could be unsealed. To her, it seemed as if her father had not yet understood how to unmake them. Gwafa Illi went to her father's desk, still holding the bowl, and as she was looking at it and thinking that its content was lovely, she suddenly felt an urge to shake it and was astonished to discover that the movement did not disturb the scene. While sitting at the desk, her eyes fell on a little doll that her father had always kept on the desk. He had bought the doll for her when she was a young child of five but he had insisted on keeping it on his desk, to be daily reminded of his beautiful daughter.

Gwafa Illi inherited all of her grandfather and father's books and research instruments. In the past, only her mother looked after the family library but after suffering a major stroke that left her partially paralysed and able to move only her right arm and the right-hand side of her face, the queen was forced to give up control and withdraw from public life. Thinking about her mother, Gwafa Illi recalled seeing her give a sigh of relief at the news that their desert was now under the protection of ONO. She sensed that it was perhaps time for her to find out why.

Gwafa Illi went to her mother's apartment taking the bowl and the doll with her. As soon as her mother saw the objects, tears fell down her cheeks. She moved her right arm as if to signal to her daughter that she had to move fast. When Gwafa Illi asked her mother if the liquid in the bowl was water, her mother opened her right-hand eye wide and spun her right hand over her head.

"Is it more than water?" her daughter asked surprised.

Her mother moved her right eyelid up and down, this was her way of saying yes.

"How is it more?"

In response to her daughter's question, the queen caressed her own face, smiling, making small movements.

"Does it rejuvenate people?"

Again her mother moved her right eyelid up and down.

"Water of longevity?"

Her mother smiled and took the hand of her daughter and kissed it.

"What else can it do?"

Her mother replied by pointing to the sky and then put her right hand in front of her eyes as if protecting them from the sun.

"Is it resistant to the sun?" Gwafa Illi shook her head in disbelief.

The mother replied with a smile.

"It does not evaporate?"

Her mother moved her right eyelid up and down.

"Where is it?"

The queen looked at her daughter seemingly disconcerted. Then she moved her hand in such a manner as if she was ploughing.

"Under the desert?"

The right-hand side of her face smiled.

"Our desert?"

Her mother smiled again. She took her daughter's hand and pressed it to signal danger and urgency.

"Do I need protection?"

Her mother moved her eyelid, then by rotating her hand she signalled again that Gwafa Illi had to hurry up. She pointed to the doll and she moved her hand from left to right as if she was unwinding something. In response to her mother's movements, Gwafa Illi turned the doll's little legs, then the arms but nothing happened. When she finally turned the head of the doll, she heard a click. She removed the head and looked inside the doll. She saw a small memory stick, probably one of the first-ever used, and after removing it, she noticed a message from her father. "Keep it safe, keep it secret." He wrote those words in a dialect that her grandparents had forced his own son to learn and that her father had forced her to learn pretending that it was one of the ancient languages of their dynasty. Gwafa Illi dutifully learned it but when she went to school, the teachers told her that no such language existed. She, however, decided to speak to her grandparents and parents only in this language, particularly when they were in the palace, and subsequently, she forced her own two children to learn it also. It was a language that excluded unwanted listeners and protected their conversations. She looked at her mother and noticed her serene features. All past worries had gone. Her beauty had returned as defiant as ever against a half-dead body.

"Did you and Dad ever try to get a drop of the water?"

Her mother smiled while pointing to the bowl and knocking on it, signalling that they had not managed to open it. Longevity had never been so close and yet it was still so far.

"Who will protect us?" asked Gwafa Illi. Her grandmother wrote three letters in the air, O-N-O. Afterwards, she seemed too exhausted to continue. Gwafa Illi embraced her and thanked her. She then called her two children and made them pay their respect to their grandmother.

In the evening, Queen Mother died in peace, knowing that she had helped her daughter understand the dangers and risks of being the new Queen in times of great change. The following day, Gwafa Illi took over the role of Queen formally, with an official investiture to follow. A short press release informed the world of the sad event, which would have passed unnoticed only three days earlier, but now that the Blue City and its desert were under the direct protection of ONO, every piece of news about them interested politicians and investors, scientists and researchers. This part of the world that not so long ago was considered inaccessible was now exciting everybody's imagination.

Once calm had returned to the capital and the palace, Gwafa Illi took the old memory stick and plugged it into her father's ancient computer. Immediately, a document opened up written by grandfather in their secret dialect. The same text then appeared in English, translated by her father who had titled it *From Ancient Algorithms to Complex Algorithms*. The text included mathematical calculations on which her grandfather had written comments in the margins. Then two long formulae followed extending over several pages. Gwafa Illi noticed that in this part of the text her father had also written some comments and in addition, referred to an appendix. Her father's comments were written half in English and half in their secret language, and when she translated the latter into English, they did not seem to make any sense. Her grandfather's writing was also impenetrable. At first, her grandfather discussed the ancient Greek mathematician Euclid and his geometric algebra, then he turned to the Persian mathematician, astronomer, and geographer Muhammad Al-Khwarizmi, known also under the Latin name Algorithmi, who lived around the ninth century. Gwafa Illi was able to follow her grandfather's argument until she came to a passage where he speculated that one day, algorithms would take the form of human bodies. She found this to be a strange idea but also thought that she was perhaps misunderstanding the text. She turned again to her father's notebook; from his notes it appeared that he had read his own father's text and judged it too risky to be published; accordingly, he decided to lock it away until his mathematics could be shared with others. She kept reading her grandfather's theory of complex algorithms sensing that it was something special, something that needed to be shared. But with whom?

While she was intent on figuring out what could have inspired her grandfather to develop what looked like a theory of algorithms, the door was thrown open and her husband stormed in. In agitated manners, he immediately enquired with her what the ONO Heritage nomination was all about. In an unflattering tone, he expressed the view that the nomination could undermine the scientific work conducted in their university or even deprive them of their capacity to use the desert as they pleased. He also asked why she had spent the last few days studying old useless papers. Gwafa Illi was taken aback by her husband's commanding tone. He had placed himself in front of her desk in an attempt to intimidate her.

"Don't forget to whom you are speaking!" Gwafa Illi replied.

"But do you realise what this protection means?"

"Again, remember to whom you are speaking," said the Queen. Then with a lack of patience that surprised also herself, she told him to leave the library.

"Next time you want to speak with me, ask first for permission."

As she finished her sentence, a guard entered the room and accompanied Amastan Badis out. She knew that he did not mean to hurt her but she felt that he had overstepped the line far too often in recent times. In the evening, Amastan Badis sent her an apology and asked for permission to speak to the Queen. She granted him permission and then the two discussed the ONO's decision. They did not understand completely why Achilles had made such a move but she concluded that if he had made it, there must have been compelling reasons.

"You seem to trust him more than everybody else."

"That's correct!" replied his wife smiling.

"Any reason why you should trust Achilles more than the people of the desert?"

"Wrong question," she replied, "you should ask: can ONO protect us in times of great change and danger?"

"Hm… I sense that you are not telling me everything."

"Have some faith."

They went out onto the terrace and turned their gaze toward the sinuous Sahara that was stretching out towards the horizon, as beautiful and secretive as ever.

Chapter 21

Wednesday morning, Achilles and his team arrived at the Longyearbyen military base. The team included Adam, Åke, Angelo, Colonel Neill, his deputy, two military experts in technological advancement, Melitus, and on remote connection the ONO director-general. Martha, George, and Roman were already at the base along with the two scientists sent by Neill. Olsen's team included his closest aides Asbjørn Larsen, Bente Hansen and Daniel Sandvig, two scientific experts, one from biochemical research and one from weaponry, and twenty soldiers. Also part of the colonel's team was Dagmar Sandberg, communication and culture minister of the Norwegian government, assisted by a representative of the secret service and a member of the police.

Olsen welcomed Achilles and his team and immediately briefed them about the latest developments concerning the waterhole in the room located at the east side of the vault. The hole had expanded a fair bit and there was fear among the scientists that biological agents such as bacteria had overspread in the area. Taking over the conversation, the scientists said that they had detected several new small holes in the floor of the vault, more precisely along the tunnel as well as near the storage area. They had carried out tests on the water samples they had managed to retrieve from the holes and the first results seemed to suggest that the holes might have been caused by corrosive substances contained in the melting water rather than by genetically enhanced bacteria. Unfortunately, the scientists added, they could not provide watertight evidence yet to support their data and as a consequence, everybody would have to wear protective gear on the following day's mission to the vault.

It was now Achilles' turn to provide some updates. He started out by reminding everybody of the classified nature of all the information he was about to share. He then explained GAIC's theory of a hidden chamber located between doors two and three. To access the hidden chamber, he said, they probably had to crack an algorithm. Achilles immediately clarified that he was not in the position to say anything about what was stored in the hidden room, because there was a high probability that except for those who had created the chamber, no one else had ever had access to it. This information left Olsen and Neill speechless.

After the updates, Olsen's soldiers brought in bread, cold fish and meat, cheese, and other tasty Nordic food, and everybody relaxed in preparation for tomorrow's mission to the vault which was to start at four o'clock in the morning. Although tension was palpable in the air, everybody tried to be as cheerful as possible. Achilles had pleasant conversations with everybody and saw Åke and Angelo engaged in a cordial exchange.

Earlier, Angelo had wondered why Achilles had wanted him to be part of this mission but now he felt happy for the trip since it had given him the opportunity to meet his old friend Åke. Achilles heard them speak joyfully about their time together at the Vatican. Everybody was relaxed and chatting away cordially. Achilles wished for better times for everybody but until the vault's issues remained unresolved, worries would prevail. Time passed quickly and gradually, one by one, everybody retired for the night. Before leaving for his room, Achilles was addressed by Olsen who informed him that his team could not find any caves in the area around the vault. He also made the comment that no seeds would have survived undamaged the cold temperature of the North Pole.

Early in the morning, four military helicopters left the Longyearbyen military base for the Svalbard vault. Two carried the civilian teams and the soldiers tasked with their protection. The other two choppers carried soldiers and military emergency instruments. On arrival, everybody put on protective gear and gloves, everybody was also asked to keep the oxygen mask included in the safety gear ready to hand. Achilles was wearing a 360-degree body camera that filmed the whole mission. No one else was allowed to record the event. Once inside the vault, the mission was under Achilles' command but he intended to share it with Olsen and Neill. Achilles was remotely connected with ONO's director-general who would step-in should something happen to Achilles.

They finally reached the vault and entered it with eagerness but also with caution and walked down the tunnel. Martha, Roman, and the other scientists were walking ahead of the teams, pointing to unsafe spots where the ground had caved in. Finally, they were standing in front of the doors to the storage hall, which were all closed. Achilles turned to Adam and gave him orders to proceed. Adam activated his program. He then made some calculations after which he pointed a strong light against the four doors; this light had the strange effect to render the four doors invisible under its strong beam. Then another light, this time darker, highlighted a space set between doors two and three where Adam supposed the hidden chamber was located. He marked the contours of that section which instantly, stood out as a fifth door. Despite the information that Achilles had imparted the night before, everybody felt overcome by emotion when the hidden door suddenly appeared.

At this point, Adam declared that he was going to try to open the hidden door and that they should be prepared for whatever followed since he could not anticipate what would happen next. Adam applied his algorithm program but at first nothing happened. Soon after, however, a soft whistle was heard which grew several decibels in a second. Finally, it came to a stop, and when this happened, the door opened so abruptly to catch them by surprise and make everybody move back. Only Åke, Achilles clearly noticed, did not react, nor did the director-general who appeared equally composed on the screen of his device.

With the door completely open, they felt a current of icy air come out of the chamber. The draft was so strong that it was impossible for them to enter the chamber. After a while, though, the flow of air came to a stop and a feeble light became visible. At first, no one moved until Åke took the initiative and walked into the chamber, immediately followed by Roman and Melitus. The chamber was deep in the ground, and to reach its middle, they had to walk down a short slope. In a few more seconds, everybody was inside.

If, before entering the hidden chamber, they had expected to find something unpleasant, such as weapons of mass destruction or frozen bodies or monsters produced in illegal experiments, the scene that awaited them inside was simply marvellous. The first thing they noticed was a platform placed in the middle of the chamber and a huge jar fastened to the base of the platform. The jar resembled an ancient amphora and seemed to be made of some of the finest glass ever seen. It contained water. The jar was hanging from a gold chain that made it look like a shining jewel, a precious pendant. The water in the jar shone intensely, it was luminous, emanating a sense of life that left Martha breathless. The scientists expressed admiration and were instantly joined in their commendation by the others. The jar was surrounded by a delicate grate made of thin material that resembled fine gold.

"Good Lord," said Roman, "look at that material, never seen anything like it. I've read a lot about research trying to get glass made of transparent silver but I thought we were still unable to produce it." Then, turned to Achilles he stated that what looked like glass was in fact a sophisticated chemical combination of water, silver, and air, known for being indestructible or at least, he said, this is how it was described in the scientific journals.

"Not even your bacteria would be able to destroy it," said Roman triumphantly addressing the bio scientists.

"It can't be very old, surely," said Achilles in reply to Roman's observations.

"Fifty, perhaps one hundred years in material development is nothing. But this is not just any kind of material. This is something very extraordinary." In saying this, Roman had moved closer to the platform but was stopped by Melitus' voice.

"This water," Melitus declared, "is not normal water. It is a new kind of water. A few drops could revitalise whole areas. One bottle could make many regions around the desert fertile, and one single drop could rejuvenate many people, making them live a thousand years." No one replied to his statement. "We must get it out of here! Do you have any ideas how precious this jar is? It's worth... it's worth more than anything else on the planet. It is the earth itself sharing its power to regenerate. It's the gift of longevity!"

The professor had spoken quickly. He was in trance. He felt joy and happiness but soon his good feelings changed and took a turn for the worse. "We could get rich, make others do what we want!" While uttering those words, he moved closer to the grate.

"I advise you to stay back!" Achilles said.

"But don't you see what we have here? This is the most valuable resource in the whole universe!"

"Don't touch that grate!" shouted Adam but it was too late. The professor had already stretched out his hand towards the grate. The grate disintegrated in a flash, and to their total amazement recomposed itself in its entirety even quicker.

"What you see is an illusion," said Adam, "it's a mathematical formula created to protect the jar."

"Beyond our reach?" asked George.

"Indeed!" exclaimed Adam. "A mathematical formula can only be destroyed by another mathematical formula. The human hand has no power against mathematics."

"Are these the weapons of the future?" Neill wondered.

"I think so."

While they were speaking, the ground began to shake, abruptly and unexpectedly, causing the platform to move dangerously and the jar swing forth and back so strongly as to give the impression it would break the golden chain that fastened it to the platform.

"Get out of here!" shouted the two colonels, giving orders to everybody to put on their oxygen masks. They began to move back except for Åke who was standing immovable in front of the jar. As soon as Angelo noticed that his friend was not retreating, he stopped and turned to Åke, shouted, "Why aren't you coming? Quick Åke, get away from there."

As Åke did not answer, Angelo decided to go over to him and help him leave the chamber. When he reached him and put his arm around the waist of his friend, Angelo noticed that Åke seemed to be in trance. At first, Angelo was surprised at the stiffness of his body but on noticing that Åke had turned his smiling gaze at him, Angelo felt reassured. "Quick, Åke, move!"

The walls in the chamber were slowly starting to crack under some extreme pressure, and the strong noise made by crushing stones mixed with the shaking of the floor added to the general panic that Åke's immobility was causing.

"Come on, Åke," called out Roman, "move your ass! Get out of here. Who is ever going to teach me unusuality if not you?"

In the meantime, Achilles had moved closer to Åke and after squeezing his shoulder with his right hand turned to Angelo.

"Åke won't come…" His warm voice cut through the cold.

"Why not?" Angelo cried.

"Don't you understand?" Adam asked at this point.

"No!" Angelo shouted.

"Well, if it is of any consolation to you, I don't get it either," said Olsen.

Angelo looked at Achilles and then at Adam. He sensed that all his Latin was letting him down. Not even his being a descendant of the Tudors was helpful. It was as if all of his knowledge was dormant just now when he needed it so desperately.

"Åke's time might have expired," declared Adam.

Everybody looked at Adam, incredulously. Was he saying that Åke was not a human being? Achilles checked the device of his screen and saw that the director-general had a passive expression on his face and realised that he had not reacted to anything during the past hour or so. He checked the time. It was ten o'clock in the morning in Svalbard and four in the morning in New York. The ground now shook so violently that it became obvious to everybody that they had to leave immediately. Achilles stretched out his arm and fetched Angelo, then everybody got quickly out of the chamber and started to walk fast towards the exit. They reached the main entrance faster than they had supposed and exited the vault without hesitation. They were now all standing outside and looking horrified at the vault when they heard Roman's voice vibrate in the air.

"Oh no, I forgot something!" And before Achilles or Olsen could react, they saw him run back into the vault. While they were staring anxiously at the entrance hoping to see Roman return, they saw a giant glacier advancing towards them. It seemed impossible that it could stop before reaching them but it did come to a sudden stop, although not before crushing the vault. They were looking at what had remained of the building when they noticed a figure emerge from the left corner of what had once been the main door and immediately fall to the ground. It was Roman. Achilles and the military medical staff ran towards him and instantly realised that he was very unwell. He was holding something in his right hand, it was the micro-cameras he had put in the room with the large waterhole and outside the storage hall. He had installed them during one of their first missions to the vault, and it was these cameras which he had gone back to retrieve. He raised his arm and placed the cameras in Achilles' hand and since Achilles had not removed his gloves and mask, it was safe for him to take them. He put the cameras in a special bag and sealed it, then holding the bag tightly, he opened a safe box and laid the bag in it. He sealed the box and transferred it to one of his rucksacks. In the meantime, Roman was helped by military doctors in protective gear to slide inside a tube that isolated him from the rest of the world, they lifted him into one of the helicopters, which took off instantly. Achilles was stunned by the speed of these actions.

No one spoke during the return trip to the Longyearbyen base and everybody was grateful that the monotony of the helicopters' rotors helped them to calm down their tumultuous feelings. Once at the base, they gathered in the main room. Angelo had not uttered a single word since their escape from the vault. They sat down and looked at each other, still in disbelief. Then Angelo turned to Adam.

"Explain it again! I have not understood anything of what has passed." Angelo's voice was trembling.

Adam replied warmly that he himself was not completely sure why Åke had behaved so oddly. "The only thing I fully understand now is that my program alone would not have opened the hidden door, that to open that door a complex algorithm was needed, which makes me think that Åke was somehow in control of such an algorithm or he might even be an algorithm himself."

"Did you suspect as much?" Angelo asked Achilles.

"I thought he might be a sort of artificial intelligence or a mix of human-computer identity," replied Achilles while recalling two occasions on which he had found some of Åke's movements unnatural.

"You never told me this," said Angelo in a sad voice.

"Does it matter who our friends are if they inspire love and friendship in us and as long as they deserve our affection?"

Olsen and Neill looked at Achilles in total amazement.

Adam went on to say that Åke might have been created several decades ago and that he was probably one of the first, if not the first, complex artificial intelligences ever built. Adam also said that unfortunately, he could not provide any evidence about what he had just said for he knew no theoretical texts he could cite to prove his point. "Mine are mere conjectures."

While they were going through all that had happened in the vault, an urgent call came in from the ONO headquarter. It was Meher. She informed Achilles that the office had experienced an emergency. At three in the morning, all lights went out and all doors automatically locked. All machines, all computers came to a stop. Those who had stayed in the office overnight for safety reasons were locked up for a whole hour. Some had been in the café helping Romeo prepare the breakfast buffet when everything went silent. Security had responded immediately. After approximately 60 minutes, normality had returned. All the laboratories that had automatically sealed their doors during the emergency were again operating properly. There had been no material risk to people and files. This last piece of information was particularly important to Achilles and he secretly hoped that the director-general had placed the box containing the plant and water, which Annabelle had found in the desert, in a secure place. He wondered about the time of the emergency and it occurred to him that it must have happened exactly when they were experiencing the earthquake in the vault.

But if Achilles and the others thought that the turbulent event at the ONO headquarter had marked the end of a historic day, they were soon to be told otherwise. News now came in from the director-general that an earthquake of the highest magnitude was recorded in the Sahara Desert, which destroyed all the archaeological excavations of the Tuaregs. All the desert faults that had appeared during the last one hundred years were now submerged under tons of sand. Immense new dunes had formed, leaving large parts of the desert inaccessible to caravans and archaeological expeditions. This piece of news left Achilles breathless.

The more Achilles thought about the events that had accompanied the theft of the seeds, the more he sensed that what, at first, had just seemed to be a number of disconnected events, had meanwhile taken the form of a distinct pattern. The Svalbard vault and its contents came to mind. Sadly, the vault was now lying under an immense glacier; ancient water had seemingly wanted to protect new water from humanity's grabbing hands. And copying the glaciers, ancient sand had taken back control over the desert, blocking human access to

172

its resources. Perhaps, the time for this new water had not yet arrived. Other issues seemed to stand between the past and the future, and those issues had to be resolved by the present.

Chapter 22

The Norwegian government and ONO informed the global community that a moving glacier had crushed the vault of Svalbard. Photographs showed a majestic glacier now standing where the vault had once stood. The bad news added to the other bad news about the stolen seeds. Not everybody seemed to be unhappy about the loss of the vault, though. Some people expressed relief at its disappearance; they had always considered the vault as a security risk, for they viewed it as a potentially dangerous entry into Scandinavia. Others suspected that a breach of security had occurred and that the government was playing it down, a suggestion that set the public in panic. Some other people spoke about tests carried out in the vault that involved the use of genetically manipulated bacteria and new viruses. Unverified reports were cited in some media about precious materials hidden in the vault behind secret doors.

It was necessary to dispel all these fears. Ironically, nothing could be revealed without adding to the rumours. Achilles did not know how to manage the expectations of the public. What would happen if new water was mentioned? And was the theory of new water correct anyway? Would not people and governments want to lay their hands on the jar?

And would not rich governments or multinationals offer trillions to get access to the ruins of the vault? What would happen if Norway admitted that there were several holes, some of very large dimensions, in the ground of the vault and whose origin was still unclear? And would not the revelation that a jar full of a new kind of water was in the vault provoke reactions that could lead to new conflicts, to a world war? These were all questions of great importance, for they impacted informed consent and ONO.

Tension was now palpable everywhere in the world and it had to be understood in order to restore confidence in the scientific work of the Nordic Alliance, especially when it came to the creation of new collections of seeds and perhaps also building of a new vault. Here Achilles received unexpected help from the Earth Movement. Its leaders made it known to him that they were prepared to reveal the whereabouts of the seeds and to do so prior to the global negotiation at which he had promised to let them explain their theft and present their manifesto for food.

The stolen seeds were handed over to the Nordic Alliance and the Norwegian government; hereafter, several scientists were invited to check their identity and status. The scientists were pleased to confirm that the returned seeds were indeed the Svalbard seeds and that they were in very good conditions. After this confirmation, the news about the retrieval of the seeds was made public. Achilles sighed. A day that had started under bad auspices, had taken an unexpected positive turn to the relief of everybody. People rejoiced at the return of the seeds and many organisations and communities were now asking to be involved in the planning and storage of the world's seeds. In response to these requests, the Nordic

Alliance in cooperation with its parent organisation the International Alliance for Agricultural Heritage made a public declaration of intents: they would initiate an open process for future collections and storages and asked ONO to assist in the creation of the next vault. As a consequence, the organisation of new seed collections and the establishment of a new vault were to follow ONO's policy of informed consent.

Chapter 23

To be back in New York after the difficult mission to the vault was a welcome change for everybody. The familiarity of the place and the warmth of its people helped the ONO team to regain its calm, despite the sadness at Åke's death, the anguish caused by Roman's hospitalisation, and the inconvenience resulting from the loss of the vault. No one in Achilles' office could think about these events without feeling deeply touched by them, something that made it difficult to focus on other tasks. After his return, Achilles asked the director-general about the whereabouts of the desert plant and water that were under his custody and was relieved to hear that they were safe. He kept thinking about the recent incidents wondering if he had perhaps overlooked something important. The tension in his mind was relentless and recurring questions troubled him. How did Åke come about? Who created him? When?

One day, while Achilles was wrestling with these unresolved questions, he received a message on his classified device. Only the director-general, Angelo, the head of the negotiators, and the head of the rhetoricians had access to it. It was a request of access coming from a code unknown to him. Achilles decided to grant it and was astonished to discover that the request came from Gwafa Illi. Achilles did not ask her how she had gotten hold of his secret number, postponing the question for the time being and focusing instead on what she had to tell him. But he clearly understood that to get through to him on that device, she must have had some very special help.

Gwafa Illi described to him the material she had found on one of her grandfather's memory sticks, mentioning also her own father's notebook in which he had tried to explain his own father's research. She informed him that her grandfather had been a student of Alan Turing and that he used to cite Turing's favourite maxim that "a computer would deserve to be considered intelligent if it could deceive a human into believing that it was human." She added that her father was also an admirer of Turing and in line with the master's teaching kept repeating that misunderstood knowledge was lost knowledge. She was now offering to send Achilles all the working notes and papers of her father and grandfather, to see if he could make sense of the files.

Achilles thanked her and expressed appreciation for her trust. He also mentioned that he would have to involve some of his scientists in reading the documents she was going to transfer. Gwafa Illi gave him permission to share her material with his scientists provided Achilles never lost control over it; she also said that she would send her files in reading mode only and with an expiry date, after which all documents would disappear from his device forever. He accepted her conditions and thanked her again. A short pause followed which he broke by asking her abruptly if she thought that there was water under the desert.

The Queen sighed. "Dad believed that there was a lake deep below the desert which in his view contained a source of exceptional water and vegetation."

"I see."

After this brief exchange, they fell silent for a moment. This was a topic which neither of them wanted to dwell on for too long out of fear of saying too much, hence, both submitted to a change of subject without any reluctance. They went on to talk about the Heritage protection bestowed by ONO and other issues of common interest and concern. When they parted, Achilles promised to get back in touch as soon as he could say something sensible about the material she was going to send him.

Thinking again about the expectations evoked by a little plant with luminous water droplets covering its leaves, he wondered if he had not been too eager to believe what Melitus had told him. His doubts made him feel uneasy but he soon recovered and looked forward to the files that Gwafa Illi had promised to send. A few minutes later, she transferred the work of her father and grandfather. Little did he know at this point, that those files would help him solve some of the mystery that still surrounded the Svalbard vault and the water jar. He hastily opened them and in noticing that they dealt with mathematics, he called Adam. It took Adam only a quick check to realise that the files contained two algorithms with very special capabilities.

"I need more time to fully understand what I'm looking at," said Adam, excited.

"Why don't you stay in my office and work through the files and let me know your conclusions? And please remember that these are classified documents."

Chapter 24

Achilles left his office and headed over to the café to enjoy Romeo's afternoon hot chocolate. While sitting on at a table discreetly located behind two plants, he found himself admiring Romeo's recent renovation of the place. He had reshuffled some of the furniture and acquired new buffet components, such as a coffee machine and fresh juice dispensers.

It had been the first renovation since the establishment of ONO. While he was observing the effects of the changes, Achilles saw the director-general enter the café. The director-general did not seem to notice Achilles. He went straight to the buffet, picked up a cup and moved over to the place where the coffee machine had stood before the renovation. He raised his left arm and made a movement as if he was pressing the coffee button, then shifted to the right and pressed where the milk button used to be. Achilles looked on horrified and was about to go over to the breakfast bar to help him when a new idea entered his mind. He remained seated and noticed that the director-general had now moved to the left, where the juice dispenser used to be, and suddenly came to a halt. Achilles kept sipping his chocolate with so serious a look that the two interns who had just entered the café and were looking at the director-general amused turned and left immediately. Not a sound was uttered by anyone. Everything was still and Achilles was waiting for something to happen. Slowly, he started to comprehend what had remained obscure to him for so long. Adam came running into the café, holding Achilles' device in his hands and talking in an agitated manner while moving towards him.

"Listen," Adam said to Achilles, "I know what the files contain. Listen to this. They are mathematical calculations used to create two complex algorithms. By this, I mean two human algorithms! You see, I think that Åke was one of those two algorithms. I can now say with absolute certainty that it was not my program that opened the door to the hidden chamber in the vault, something I had long suspected but wasn't able to prove until now. The algorithm protecting that chamber was too difficult for my little brain. What I was able to create instead was a program capable of detecting the presence of some new algorithms. This is wonderful knowledge! It will revolutionise everything!" Adam continued to say that he was now in the position to draw more conclusions about complex algorithms.

Achilles did not reply. In his mind, he was pulling threads together, matching ends and waiting for something to reveal itself. He turned to Adam and noticed that he was now scanning the files on his device, totally enchanted by what he saw. After a long while, Adam seemed to notice what was going on at the buffet.

"What is the DG meaning by standing there in such a stupid manner?"

"His time is up," said Achilles. But Adam did not seem to register his answer. At this point, the director-general turned around and came over to Achilles. Adam looked at him and then lost himself again in his device.

"Well, Achilles, I have taken leave. I feel exhausted and need a break," said the director-general, "not sure when I'll be back. You will have to look after this place. It has been such a pleasure to meet you, I didn't expect humans to be very smart but you are special."

Achilles smiled. The director-general stretched out his hand, catching him by surprise. Achilles instantly remembered what he had once said to Angelo, "Does it matter who your friends are if they inspire you in good ways?"

Achilles rose and returned the handshake. In the meantime, Adam had regained control and on noticing the director-general rose also, although abruptly.

"I wish you well, Adam," said the director-general, "don't be afraid of what you are," he added and after squeezing Adam's shoulders, left.

Achilles sat down again and finished his chocolate while sorting out his emotions and trying to better understand the new reality of the world. He now realised that he had never seen the director-general eat food. He always saw him only with fluids. "How silly of me not to have tried to figure out why!"

Achilles thought of Adam. Was he not too always with some fluid in his hand but never with solid food? He thought back to the night when they arrived at the Longyearbyen military base in Svalbard; after the preliminaries and the updates, the team members had shared a dinner. He had noticed that Adam had declined all kind of food but he, Achilles, had concluded that Adam might have been feeling the tension of the upcoming mission.

After a few minutes' silence on both sides, Adam resumed talking and in pointing to the screen of his device cried out, "Look, there is a complex algorithm in our office!"

"Keep an eye on that guy, Adam. Will you?"

As Achilles rose, Adam too stood up and went over to the bar to get some coffee and juice. Then while chatting jovially, he followed Achilles out of the café and turned left walking fast towards his room.

"Sir," Angelo addressed Achilles while he was walking into his office, "the DG just came by and left a parcel for you on your desk."

"Did he speak to you before leaving?"

"Yes," Angelo replied happily, "he came over to me and the junior secretaries and interns and announced his departure. He said that his time was up and that another person like him would soon follow. He complimented us on our excellent work and told us to stay focused and work hard and to not be afraid of anything, to accept who we are and always make good use of our faculties and abilities. He then hugged us and left. It was quite an emotional experience. He was always so gentle and respectful."

Achilles went into his room and saw a beautifully wrapped present on the desk. He opened it with great curiosity. He found a photograph framed in precious glass that reminded him of the glass jar in the vault of Svalbard. It was a picture of all the members of the GAIC's office in which everybody was smiling, and since it was a digital live photograph, he saw them chatting and moving around happily. Achilles held it in his hand and then for some inexplicable reason, he shook it. The first image immediately disappeared letting a new scene emerge. There he saw the little plant, its leaves covered with the water droplets; it was lying in a sandbank submerged in the shining water from the desert. As he was admiring the scene, Angelo popped in.

"Sir, Romeo is taking us to a restaurant downtown where he says the food is 'squisitissimo'. Everybody is coming, even the negotiators and rhetoricians. Will you join us?"

"Sure."

The evening passed in harmony. The negotiators and rhetoricians were outstanding in keeping the conversations and chats going; always inscrutable, due to their roles, they had skills many could only dream of and could interact with everybody without ever judging or giving the impression of censoring what was said. Towards the end of the evening, Romeo rose and holding his glass said in a joyous voice, "Colleagues, let's pay our tribute to friendship. May it always guide our decisions and infuse our sentiments."

Chapter 25

A new director-general had now to be elected and among the candidates nominated by all ONO's staff members, Adam was the favourite. Incidentally, he was elected with unanimous consent and started his work immediately. The nomination was later endorsed by all representatives of the member states. Needless to say that Adam's scientific leadership and personal style had impressed everybody from the first day of his joining ONO and GAIG. His approach to things and people was not much different from that of the previous director-general and like his predecessor, Adam attended all meetings dealing with ONO's priorities. He listened carefully to all positions when the opinions were discordant and always committed himself to resolving all issues that required his approval without any delay. Hence, the change of the director-general was more nominal than substantial. Adam certainly projected a different image through his dynamic appearance and the body of an athlete. Adam and Achilles worked very well together. No material alteration occurred in the decision-making structure, where Achilles was the main driver of change and the director his absolute supporter. As director-general, Adam was now the public face of ONO at all political and diplomatic events.

Two weeks after the failed mission to the Svalbard vault, Achilles received a request for a remote meeting from Colonel Olsen and Colonel Neill. In accepting the invitation, Achilles decided to include Adam, George and Martha in the conversation. After expressing his pleasure in seeing them all, with Neill nodding his assent, Olsen explained that he had been able to find out more information about the firm that had installed the security system in the vault. The firm was called Enigma Code and had been established in the 1950s by a group of engineers who had studied in the United States and the United Kingdom. The owner was a mathematician of northern Africa descent. The firm had a construction subsidiary that was later involved in building some parts of the vault. In 1970, Enigma Code and its subsidiary were sold to a British security company and afterwards it changed ownership several more times before being bought up by the Norwegian security firm that had been in charge of the vault's security until recently.

While listening to Olsen, Achilles gained some further insights into the history of the vault. He seemed inclined to believe that the founder and owner could have been Gwafa Illi's father who might have been supported by her grandfather. Achilles decided not to mention this to the others until he had asked her about it. He, therefore, merely observed that it must not have been too difficult for the mathematicians and engineers working for the original security firm to build the hidden chamber and install two security systems, one for the vault and its storage hall and one for the hidden chamber.

As the colonels did not seem to have anything else to add, Achilles took over the conversation.

"I believe that the people who were responsible for the construction and safety of the vault were the same people who built the hidden chamber, put the water jar in there and created the complex algorithms that protected the jar." Achilles received no comments from his listeners. Everybody seemed intent on trying to anticipate his conclusions.

"So," continued Achilles, "two issues need resolving. The first concerns CAs, the complex algorithms. If it was possible for those engineers to create CAs that protected the jar, it must also have been possible to create CAs with the opposite goal, and by this, I mean CAs that could steal the jar. Not every engineer employed in that firm might have been guided by good intentions or objectives. Indeed, some might have had other plans for that precious liquid."

Achilles looked around and noticed that everybody agreed.

"Now, I would like you to pay attention to one sequence of the film I took with my body camera during the last mission to the vault and which captured the moment Åke suddenly froze." In saying this, Achilles played the sequence on a large screen that he had hanging in his office. Everybody carefully watched the segment of the film. Melitus was speaking in an agitated manner about the new water, he then suddenly grabbed the grate with his hands causing it to disintegrate. Achilles asked his colleagues to tell him what they had just seen. Everybody repeated the same story: Melitus speaking, grabbing the grate and destroying it. Achilles played the segment again and again and everybody saw the same events unfold. Eventually, realising that they were unable to see what he saw, he urged them to think back to what had happened in the vault.

"Remember what Adam said about the grate?" asked Achilles. "Only a mathematical formula can destroy another mathematical formula. Now we know or we assume that Åke embodied an algorithm and that the moment he was killed or perhaps just put out of order was precisely the moment at which the grate disintegrated. Do you follow me?" Achilles noticed the concentrated looks of Olsen and Neill.

"Remember that, if it is true that only maths can stop maths, then there was more than one algorithm in the vault that day. Now, please watch the film segment again. It took me long to see what really happened." Achilles' hint had the effect of increasing the alertness of the others and this time, they clearly saw Melitus grab the grate and hit Åke. The action happened so fast to be easily overlooked, now, however, they could see what truly happened. While all of this was taking place, Achilles, probably caught by surprise, had moved back or sideways, causing his body camera to shift focus, nonetheless, it captured something extraordinary. Melitus was suddenly not on the film recording, to reappear only a few seconds later. Since everybody was busy looking at the grate, Melitus' absence passed unnoticed.

"Good Lord," said Olsen, "what happened?"

Achilles turned to Adam who in the meantime had learned a lot from the files sent by Gwafa Illi.

Adam took over the conversation, "Melitus embodied the formula that used the grate to destroy Åke."

"Was he an enemy CA?" Neill asked.

"If you want to use military language, then yes, we might have witnessed a battle between algorithms."

"And the good one, Åke, lost out?"

"Probably."

188

Adam reminded them that there was nothing they could have done for Åke for only mathematicians can revive an algorithm.

"But why was Åke unable to protect himself?"

"We can only guess for now," replied Adam. "Åke needed us to get to the vault since a complex algorithm could not have travelled to Svalbard and gone to the vault on its own. CAs always need humans to get going, for they appropriate the rational goals of human beings and act within the boundaries of those goals. Through our goal, we gave Åke the opportunity to get into the vault and at the same time, we gave the same opportunity to Melitus, who, however, for some reason later turned against Åke."

Adam now addressed Achilles. "Didn't you mention two issues?"

Before answering, Achilles called Angelo and asked him to contact Melitus at his university. Achilles signalled to the others that he wanted to wait for Angelo to get back to him before resuming the conversation.

"Sir, I've been told that Professor Melitus is nowhere to be found and has been missing for the past two weeks."

Achilles thanked Angelo and addressed Adam's question.

"So, let me add some data to the pattern we need to understand. Complex algorithms need humans to carry out their tasks, in other words, human beings prepare the conditions for CAs to act according to their design, which is the result of complex mathematical formulae. Åke needed us to get to the vault and inside the vault. His job was to protect the water. Let's assume he's dead…"

"Is he not?" Olsen asked.

"Let's assume he's dead," Achilles pressed ahead, "and that his opponents have won. But how are they going to get the water jar out of the vault or better still, how did they get it out?"

"What! Is it not buried under stones and ice?" Neill's surprise equalled that of the others.

"Is it?" replied Achilles crossing his arms and reverting to his inscrutable look.

"I can't imagine anything else since the whole vault collapsed when the stones came crushing down," said George.

"Have you ever heard of the hidden ocean?" Achilles asked suddenly.

"Yes," said Martha with a look that revealed her surprise at how quickly Achilles picked up new information. "It's an ocean that lies under the Atlantic Ocean and is called the Arctic Ocean. Information about it is scattered but satellite pictures and modelling suggest that it's connected with the North Pole. It is said to be very deep, almost reaching the centre of the earth."

"More can be said about it," continued Achilles, "because there seems to exist a mild current that turns the Arctic Ocean warmer during certain periods of the year, which is why it used to be called the Arctic Mediterranean Sea, and some scientists still call it that way. Keep in mind that warm water is lighter than icy water and easier to travel through," Achilles paused briefly and then resumed his talk speedily.

"From a geographical viewpoint, the Arctic Ocean forms a cul-de-sac through the Bering Strait and the land masses that surround its basin in the Northern Hemisphere. It is, however, open to the outside via a piece of land deep in the Atlantic Ocean that lies between Greenland and Scandinavia. Current data and scientific modelling suggest that the floor of the Arctic Ocean is immense and that its basin communicates with the Scandinavian Basin which is, however, smaller. The basin of the Arctic Ocean stretches across the Svalbard Archipelago to Norway, Iceland, and Greenland. There seems to be a corridor that connects the waters of these countries and which scientists think has the form of a narrow seabed furrow called the Lena Trough. In some places, this seabed is 4,000 metres or 1400 feet deep. The Scandinavian Basin is filled with the waters of the Arctic Ocean and it is open to the Atlantic through channels on both side of Iceland. Exit to the wide oceans occurs in two ways, deep down from the Norwegian Sea towards the Atlantic or on the surface via the Greenland and Labrador Currents."

Achilles saw how Olsen and Neill changed expressions. A whole world of possibilities was opening up in their minds.

"It would be a logistic nightmare for anyone to go to Svalbard that way, wouldn't it?" a nervous Olsen asked.

"It would certainly be so for human beings," replied Achilles.

"But not for artificial intelligence or complex algorithms?" asked George.

"But don't they need people to get to where they have been designed to go and operate accordingly?" interjected Neill.

"Yes," replied Achilles, "and that's our next major issue here."

"But why would anyone invest money or resources to do so?"

"Think of the bounty," replied Achilles. "If that water is really what has been suggested, durable and making people live longer, then anyone possessing it could rule the world. That water would beat genetics if it could be replicated!"

"Good Lord," said Olsen, "this goes beyond my military experience and comprehension."

No one replied. They weighed the possibilities without censuring anything, for they had already witnessed so much since the theft of the seed from the Svalbard vault and the discovery of the water jar that they were in no mood to discount what even now seemed to be quite impossible.

Achilles pressed ahead with his interpretation of what might have happened after they ran out of the vault. "Even if the hidden Arctic Ocean were involved, and even if we were able to understand how the jar was carried out of the vault, assuming it was taken out of the vault, I still can't figure out what happened afterwards. This bit will always remain difficult to sort out." A few seconds' silence followed.

In breaking it, Olsen resumed the conversation. "Suppose things are like that then it was risky for us to be in the vault, no? What is your take?" He turned to Neill.

"I agree with you, and like you, I cannot see the whole picture. We did experience the vault and the algorithms, didn't we?"

"We did," replied Adam.

"Could something bad have happened to us?"

"I believe that we encountered scientific algorithms and not combative ones, and in that we were lucky. Had they been the latter, we would all be dead by now," said Adam.

"But would not a combative algorithm also need humans with rational goals to become active?" Olsen replied.

"For a combat algorithm to get into the vault it would have required somebody in the teams to have combative goals.

Perhaps, there were combative algorithms in the vault or in the hidden chamber but they could not be activated because, as I said, none of us had any combative goals at that time. As I mentioned earlier, in the vault we witnessed maths, namely Professor Melitus, opposing other maths, namely Åke. But I don't believe that they were designed to be combative."

"But are not combative CAs also mathematics?" George asked.

"Yes, but they can only be destroyed by other combative algorithms. Their goal, which is what they have been designed for, is to kill humans."

"Let me see if I can piece it together," said Neill, "combative CAs can only be stopped by other combative CAs, military maths by other military maths, so to speak. They can also kill humans but to do so they need humans with a rational goal to kill other humans, am I right?"

"Yes," Adam replied.

A disquieting silence followed Adam's confirmation, which was broken by him.

"Åke and Melitus' goal was to go into the hidden chamber, which is what we also wanted, yes?" Adam looked at Achilles who nodded. "So," continued Adam, "we took the two of them there. Just as we achieved our goal, which was to enter the hidden chamber, so did they!"

"But why did Melitus hit Åke?" Olsen asked.

"I believe but please consider it a conjecture at this stage," answered Adam, "that one of us expressed a goal to take the water out of the hidden chamber and get rich and that rational wish was immediately picked up by Melitus who strengthened by such human goal, struck Åke. Since Åke was guided by other human goals, I suppose, he was clearly opposed to the removal of the jar." Adam added that anyone in the vault could have influenced Melitus and that it could have been one of the scientists, one of the soldiers, the official representatives, the police or someone from ONO, namely anyone with such a goal. This information deeply unsettled everyone.

"If we could only know what happened once we ran out of the vault..." Achilles was musing aloud, "we would be able to decide whether the amphora containing that splendid water is buried under the glacier or whether through some intervention it slid down the bank into the oceans. Until we have an answer to this question, we'll never be able to confirm or deny the whereabouts of new water, let alone its very existence."

With these words, Achilles ended the meeting. He reminded the others of the upcoming global negotiation. He told them that the Earth Movement would also attend and make a declaration about the theft of the Svalbard seeds. Other expected delegates included Artists, Atheists, Churches and Free Religious Associations, Climate Scientists, the Coalition of Humanists, the Farmers League, First Nations and People, Governments, the IBEF Representation, Minorities, Mount View University, Massachusetts Institute of A.I., Members of the General Public, The New African Union, Radical Freedom, Urban Dwellers, Young Ecology. These organizations and people, Achilles said, would represent All Interests and speak in their name.

Achilles and ONO's director-general had decided that since new water was considered classified material it was not going to be part of the negotiation. It was classified because the very nature of the water was still unclear. Was it really new water? Was it healing water? Could it give longevity to humans? What else could it do? If left to the fantasy and enterprising mind of influencers such questions would throw the world into a spin; a spin, Achilles feared, that could spark a wave of explorations, some even violent, which could perhaps equal an invasion of Svalbard.

Chapter 26

The day of the global negotiation 'Humanity versus Climate Change' finally arrived and everybody sighed with relief. The Director-General and Achilles warmly welcomed All Interests, ONO's special guests and honorary members, and the media. Once all organisational preliminaries were dealt with, the representatives of All Interests moved swiftly to the places and areas assigned to them, and so did all the other numerous attendees. Everybody seemed eager to contribute to the debate, everybody wanted to influence the discourse. The organisation that more than anyone else had pleaded with Achilles for a global negotiation was the Coalition of Humanists. In recognition of its active role in having strongly pressed in favour of a global negotiation and ensured the participation of other major and minor organisations, even of those that opposed its position, the Coalition of Humanists was given the opportunity to set the main agenda of the gathering. The Coalition asked GAIC to help All Interests to achieve informed consent in three issues: the adoption of a neutral language to modulate the general debate on climate change, a more scientific discussion of the causes and impact of climate change, and the creation of an action plan for future initiatives.

In presenting their position, representatives of the Coalition of Humanists argued that due to hysteria and lack of normative guidance, recent discussions about climate change had taken on a misanthropic tone, particularly through expressions such as man-made or human-made or humanity-made disasters, and that such language could be used to create enemies and target individuals. Misanthropic language could lead to punitive actions against people as a kind of private punishment, which would be deplorable, not just illegal. All other parties attending the negotiation were asked to respond to the concerns expressed by the Coalition of Humanists.

Climate change scientists were the first to speak. While rejecting all forms of violence, they also emphasised the importance of an anti-humanist language for it helped, in their view, to identify those who had caused climate change or had influenced the climate far beyond what was scientifically believed to be naturally occurring climatic adjustments and changes. There was no danger, they said, in speaking of man-made or human-made climate change, for these expressions reflected the existing state of affairs. This position attracted criticism from the non-manufacturing communities which invoked their 'industrial innocence,' as they expressed it. They declared that the language of man-made, human-made or humanity-made needed to be integrated with the word 'white' since climate change, they argued, was white-man made. In response to this argument, some groups pointed to emerging economies that were now polluting more than western countries which would make the addition of the word white appear wrong or even discriminatory.

For their part, the group of the Governments agreed with the coalition's request because they also feared that some climate defenders could take the law into their hands and go after perceived culprits. Members of the powerful Industrial Business Economic Financial Representation, known as IBEFR, did not oppose the coalition's request either, wondering aloud, "Who else but humans can solve the problems caused by previous generations?" Scientists from the technological field noted the inadequacy of homo-centrism on both sides and rejected the language issue altogether. They emphasised that artificial intelligence could soon provide solutions to problems created by climate change. The various positions were stated carefully but they nonetheless showed strongly opposing views.

"The problem," said one of the representatives of the Coalition of Humanists, "lies in the very expressions man-made or human-made which are truly nonsensical when used to condemn human beings and shouldn't be part of any scientific or media language. It's obvious that every activity carried out by human beings is a human activity and to single this out would imply that there are activities that are not human, which is bizarre." The representative made a brief pause and then resumed talking by shifting from a philosophical consideration to a practical one. "Until we have proof that climate can indeed be influenced by humans, we really don't understand why humans should be made responsible for fires and floods, rising water, melting ice, and so forth. Have not natural catastrophes always existed? Besides, how much of a human contribution could there be? And anyway, if climate can be influenced by humans and as suggested endangering the earth, can then the earth still be considered an independent part of the universe?" The Farmers League agreed with these observations but, at the same time, its members were worried about agribusiness that in their view was mistreating the ground: "Industrialists don't know how to treat the soil, which is why draughts are occurring."

A scientist supporting climate change research made a critical observation. "Our simulations and data show distinct patterns of human influence on the climate, which is why our age has been called the Anthropocene to highlight the impact of humans on the planet, that is, the impact of human supremacy." Other scientists were seen nodding vigorously.

But the scientific community was less in agreement than what this silent approval seemed to indicate. In fact, soon after this exchange, representatives of other scientific disciplines such as evolutionary biology and biochemical palaeontology seemed to distance themselves from the environmentalists.

"Ecology has always been changing. Some life forms disappear, new ones emerge, animals adapt and so do plants. We assume that this is the same for the body of the earth," stated an evolutionary biologist.

"Aren't the changes we are witnessing too quick and revolutionary for evolution?" asked another scientist.

"We might need to establish by informed consent how to understand the word 'change'," replied a historian arguing for the Coalition of Humanists, "because some might see bad change where others see change with potential."

"Are you suggesting," intervened a representative of the Earth Movement, "that the melting of glaciers and permafrost, in general, is good for humanity? And would not water that is released cause floods everywhere and destroy human and animal habitats?"

"You people believe that the melting of ice and the rise of waters will happen in five minutes and are creating panic and hysteria by just seeing problems and never the solutions to them!" This time it was a member of the IBEFR to speak. "It's obvious that before all that frozen water melts away, we will have the solutions needed to solve the problems. Have not humans always imagined only the kind of problems they can address?"

"We know how you entrepreneurs solve problems," interjected the representative of the Earth Movement, "by creating new ones with all your technologies and inventions."

"And what about coal?" cried somebody from the back row.

"Why don't you guys go back to writing with ink and quills rather than using the devices and technologies that we have created?" another member of the IBEF Representation replied, visibly annoyed. Then turned to the person who had shouted against the use of coal said, "What in the past destroyed the woods all over Europe were fireplaces lit to warm people's houses and dwellings until coal was discovered! The hated coal, my dear fellow, saved more trees and forests than you can ever imagine! And anyway, we are now looking into new types of energies and giving people their own private batteries to store individually collected energy if this is what you guys want. Soon everybody will have their own grid at home. How about that?"

"Why should there be a problem if the ice were to melt? Would it not free up land and give us more water?" asked a government representative.

"The water originating from melting ice," replied John Delafort, "might be contaminated with ancient viruses and bacteria for which we have no remedies." He was attending the negotiation with Claire Carlie and a group of scientists who carried out climate research in an interdisciplinary manner by cooperating with archaeologists, anthropologists, historians, and geographers.

"Well, let's develop drugs against those ancient microbes and purify the water. We will be able to create artificial intelligence capable of cutting short the long shadow cast by the past!" exclaimed the representative of Mount View University. "Artificial intelligence can help create good conditions for the present and great opportunities for the future."

"But why not use your technology to explore what the earth can still give us?" Claire asked, speaking for the first time. "There might be resources that we are not yet aware of because humans have stopped imagining that there might be more to be discovered." Claire paused as if she was debating with herself whether she should mention what was on her mind and resolving the issue, continued by stating that we might all have misunderstood our planet. "Perhaps, the earth is not just round but also deep and extended into space in ways that we have never considered before, which makes me think that it must have resources such as different water or more nutrient food, that we still don't know about and that could sustain humans for another million years."

This statement had a major impact on all the people attending, included Achilles and Adam. Claire was not some junior scientist. She had been studying and researching earthly phenomena since she was a teenager. Her scientific work was widely respected, even by those who disagreed with her position on the present issue. She was saying that there might exist an unknown aspect of the earth and that new thinking was necessary to unveil it, something like the next level after homo sapiens, something that would have to be carried out by new humans.

"We certainly need to protect the earth that was originally given to us, and if some improvement is necessary, we need to make sure that it is carried out responsibly," declared the ethicist representing various groups such as spiritual communities, urban dwellers, singles, families and pensioners. It was a good remark, spoken softly and at the right moment, well received by everybody since everybody could understand it as they pleased.

Soon the negotiation would start. The rhetoricians would summarise the positions laid out in the debate. They would help the parties to resolve the issues at stake and choose informed consent as their guiding principle. The negotiators would intervene only if mediation between the parties became necessary, a task that rhetoricians, by being absolutely neutral, would never be able to carry out.

The head rhetorician moved towards the space assigned to the Coalition of Humanists and after summarising their requests, pointed out that consensus should be reached on three issues: the language of climate change, factual and perceived causes and effects of climate change, and future climate policies. The head rhetorician asked the attendees whether they would agree to the use of a language that was devoid of overt and covert judgmental terms. Several groups seemed disinclined to remove all references to humans. The Churches and religious groups attending the negotiation seemed convinced that humans were destroying the earth that God had given them, while environmentalists viewed the coalition's request as an attempt to remove responsibility. "Who would be the culprits then?" they asked.

"Why is it important to identify precise people as culprits?" asked the rhetorician.

"Is that not the only way to stop those who endanger the earth?" one of the representatives of the Earth Movement replied.

"I take from what you have just said that you are not thinking about individuals but rather bigger agents?"

"Sometimes single individuals are the culprits and sometimes whole industries and at some other times corrupt governments!"

"I've heard," said the rhetorician, "that the Aboriginal Martu, who live in the Australian Great and Little Sandy Deserts, burn desert vegetation and hunt animals. And yet their history shows that when they abandoned their deserts to join community settlements, some animals went extinct and plants disappeared but when they returned to burn and hunt again, equilibrium was restored. Does this not prove that ecology encompasses human beings with all their survival practices?"

"We speak of industrialised human beings," replied a member of a group called Radical Freedom.

"I see!" replied the rhetorician. "But now I wonder whether the expression man-made and human-made are not too detached from what an industry does or how governments operate, for those expressions seem to encompass everybody and nobody."

"We accept no industrial guilt!" shouted somebody from the area allocated to the communities of the First Nations and People and from the group of the Minorities.

"Did you hear that comment?" asked the head rhetorician facing the representatives who had rejected the coalition's request to avoid judgmental language in climate change debates and research. No one replied to her question and the silence further exacerbated the disagreement emerging from the debate. Addressing directly the groups and individuals that opposed the coalition's proposal, the head rhetorician asked them how they would reconcile their overall position about humanity being a culprit with the position taken by unindustrialised communities and minorities. "Are you not colonising the word humanity?"

"By identifying responsibility," interjected the ethicist, "attitudes can be changed."

"How far can we stretch such responsibility?" asked the rhetorician. "Are the workers in an industry to be blamed for polluting a river, are they responsible for the pollution? Certainly, workers know what happens when they carry out their tasks. And should an employee, a manager, an investor, be responsible also?"

"Investors are certainly responsible," replied the ethicist, "for they can control where their money goes. But a worker and an employee do not control the flow of work."

"You have just excluded a big piece of humanity, haven't you?" asked the rhetorician. "Is responsibility determined by what we can control or by what we know about the work we do?" In saying this, the rhetorician moved closer to the space allocated to the IBEF Representation, which was situated next to the technology scientists and the representatives of Mount View University and the Massachusetts Institute of A.I.

"Well, it's obvious that when algorithms are executing tasks, they're following a design but I would certainly not claim that an A.I. carries responsibility for the effects of, say, climate change!" exclaimed the rector of Mount View

University. "At the same time," warned the rector, "it's possible that in a not-too-distant future the term humanity might not be large enough to include new agents of artificial intelligence such as robots."

After a short pause, during which no further comments were made, the rhetorician returned to the question of responsibility. She suggested that it might be difficult, although not always impossible, to identify an individual's exact degree of responsibility when it comes to climate change, and because of that, she continued, it might well be advisable to adopt a more neutral language in talking about climate change. On a more general level, she added, it would also be advisable to proceed with great care. "As nothing is uncaused," declared the rhetorician, "climate change must be caused rather than made. By being caused, it is also subject to events that could be beyond human control. Given this state of affairs, it might be possible to grant the coalition's request to purge the language of misanthropic overtones."

In further elaborating on her viewpoint, the rhetorician mentioned something she called the chain of causality – "that is the cause that causes the next cause and the next one and so forth" – and urged general caution. The exhortation to be cautious was welcomed by everybody. A final agreement was reached between the parties that the language of climate must reflect cautionary principles. The agreement required that any future initiatives concerning the language of climate change must be grounded in informed consent.

The head rhetorician now turned to the factual and perceived causes and effects of climate change. Judging from the debate about the language, she anticipated a difficult exchange. In addition to the coalition's application requesting more circumspection with regard to the causes of climate change, the Earth Movement had filed a motion that water had to become priority number one in all the policies designed to counter the effects of climate change. The other representatives were split between these two positions. In setting the agenda for the global negotiation, the members of the Coalition of Humanists argued that clear evidence of a direct link between human activity and extreme events such as droughts, loss of agricultural land, fires, rising waters through melting permafrost, and intense monsoon rains and floods, was still missing. Perception and reality were diverging because contrary to what it was suggested by some people "a fully deterministic link might never be clearly established".

In responding to this statement, the head rhetorician invited reflection on how the earth came about. "Is not the birth of the planet earth itself a product of collisions and frictions, gases and dust, fires and rocks, and prolonged bad weather?"

"Yes, but it was followed by a long period of stability that helped to establish life and let it flourish for four and a half billion years," replied a palaeontologist.

"Well, you guys seem to like the notion of evolution so much that all the violent crises and changes that happened during that period of alleged stability are conveniently overlooked," responded a technology scientist.

"Are today's natural events, which evidently ruin many people's resources, perhaps not so totally new? Are they not already described in the oldest religious books and by early historians? Droughts, fires, polluted rivers, famines, earthquakes, etcetera are part of nature's tragic repertoire, are they not?" asked the rhetorician. She indefatigably pressed ahead, "What has really changed: climate or our perception of the effects of climate?"

"We can only speak about what we materially experience," replied a representative of the Earth Movement, "and our current experience tells us that there is a problem with the climate, that there are causes for this problem and that the ultimate effects of the problem would be a deterioration of water, which is our main resource."

"Fires are also a problem," cried somebody from the back rows.

"As are extreme weather, cyclones, and hurricanes and so forth, all caused by climate change!" shouted someone else.

"Is it not so," interjected the rhetorician, "that in some areas of the desert conditions have improved thanks to a retreat of the sand and an increase in rain, and doesn't this mean that the effects of climate change can vary?"

"One would have to examine the true causes of that improvement carefully. Is that rain as an effect of climate change? And are new agricultural techniques helping to push back the sand?" asked an environmentalist.

"Assuming techniques have improved, would they be enough to explain the retreat of the desert?" asked a member of the New African Union.

"Without water, these mightn't be long-term improvements," said Claire.

"Why are we not capturing the rains before they turn into floodwaters and use them to irrigate land, counter drought, and extinguish fires?" said a member of the IBEF Representation.

"This needs to be organised, right?, and that costs money and requires specialised labour," replied the Governments.

"And why are you not investing in such infrastructure and calling for projects from us then?" retorted a member of the industry visibly disturbed by the politicians.

"What about the melting permafrost?" asked a member of the communities living on small islands. "Will it not cause enormous problems to us islanders?"

"Land will be freed too. Is this not what happened when all the frozen water of the ice age melted away liberating land from all that useless cold?" replied a representative from the group of the Urban Dwellers.

"Is not the ice of the North Pole a reservoir of freshwater?" asked the farmers.

"It'll take centuries for the permafrost to melt. The area is the size of a continent. It won't melt all of a sudden, right? Leaving people plenty of time to resettle on new land and distil that freshwater." The industry representative spoke directly to the islanders.

"And anyway, what is all this fuss about permafrost being a reservoir of freshwater if it is poisoned by nasty viruses and bacteria? Just let it melt away!" Urged another member of the industry group.

"The melting away of the permafrost is what might free ancient microbes, viruses, and bacteria," said John in a slightly impatient tone.

"Not all viruses are enemies though," said a representative of the scientific and medical research group, "just remember that approximately eight percent of the human genome is made up of remnants of retroviruses and that the genes that form the human placenta originated from an ancient retroviral infection."

"It seems that water is the main issue here," declared the ethicist.

"A new earth will have new water!" shouted somebody from one of the back rows. "Let's find that water!"

Achilles and other members of his office looked towards the corner from where the statement had come, and so did Olsen and Neill but they could not identify the person who had made it. As the debate came to an end, it was evident to everybody that it had highlighted seemingly irreconcilable positions. But the rhetoricians did not feel intimidated by what lay ahead. They sensed that consent might be difficult to reach but not impossible. For this reason, the head negotiator, in consultation with the head rhetorician, decided to adjourn the negotiation until the following day to allow everybody to prepare for the final debate.

Chapter 27

When on the following day the negotiation resumed the tensions of the previous meeting returned with equal intensity. The question concerning the effects of climate change was still unresolved as was the more speculative issue of water. To create consensus around these matters was the task of the rhetoricians. After giving a précis of the positions, the head rhetorician started the negotiation by wondering what would happen to social life if human development and progress were to stop or even scale back. "Would this force a return to the simple life?"

"Yes," interjected a member of the Earth Movement.

"But it would be a hard life, wouldn't it," continued the rhetorician, undeterred by the assertive tone of that interjection, "for simple life could mean living without the technology that has so nicely replaced hard work. Therefore, if a simple life equals a hard life, no one would want it, right? And surely no one would want to go back to candlelight and ink. Given this understandable resistance, an important question arises; how do we keep the comforts of inventions and at the same time mitigate some of their impact, which I suppose was unpredictable before their application. Now that more studies have pointed to a critical connection between some industrial and technological activity and harm to the earth and humans, things look different but we might still be dealing here with unintentional harm as a whole. Can we accept that where harm is unintentional responsibility is difficult to assess?"

"How about intentional harm?" asked a representative of the nonindustrial communities and minorities.

"In that case, the degree of intentionality must be established and once this has been done, wrongs and grievances must be redressed through informed consent wherever possible," replied the rhetorician. "But you can certainly see that climate change is not the sole result of an agent acting independently," she continued sensing that she was still not close to a consensus. "If we consider climate change as the sum of known and unknown causes, some of which are related to human activity and some of which are not, then the effects of negligent behaviour become more or less unpredictable. And if this is the case, are you ready to adopt a different attitude towards how we understand the impact of climate change?" No one seemed in the mood to reply to her question which was in fact directed to everybody.

Pressing ahead with the negotiation, the rhetorician advanced her first proposition. "Working on making precise predictions of risks, or precise enough, could be the first task to be shared among all interested groups, yes? And it should not be too difficult to get informed consent on how to do this job, am I right?" As no opposition was voiced, it seemed that the task of reaching consensus among all the parties with regard to this question was close to being resolved. The rhetorician's second proposition followed instantly. "So if human beings cannot predict with total precision the risks originating from their activity, the question now is whether they will ever be able to predict with total precision the effects of climate change. All Interests will cooperate and let themselves be guided by informed consent in ascertaining the real, imaginary and perceived impact of climate change."

In uttering these latter words, the rhetorician had raised her voice, creating a sense of disorientation among the listeners. "Accepting this possibility, we should be prepared to acknowledge that it is unforeseeable how climate change might develop." This time she spoke in a low-pitched voice but the body language accompanying her words invested them with a dramatic tone. Silence followed, which was broken a few seconds later by the rhetorician herself. She invited the parties to acknowledge that to build common ground goodwill was necessary, and that more work had to be done to identify realistic solutions, and that cooperation should be the principle of goodwill. Everybody accepted these propositions and an agreement was drafted by All Interests that set informed consent as the main goal of any future policy development. The rhetorician had achieved an important result and afterwards, she withdrew leaving the next issue to her deputy.

The negotiation now turned to the motion filed by the Earth Movement about the centrality of water. The deputy head rhetorician, assisted by several of his senior and junior aides, laid out his ideas.

"We know that earth and water are very close elements, still no one knows for sure how water originally came to the planet earth. Would you all agree with this assessment?"

Without waiting for a reply, the rhetorician urged reflection about the possibility that water might one day disappear as mysteriously as it had first appeared on the earth. "We certainly don't need all that salty water, no?"

"Sea animals do," said a marine biologist.

"Let's assume that one day all seawater will disappear. The change would not be immediate and the marine fauna would probably be able to adapt to whatever follows. Perhaps a recreation of similar salty conditions conducive to the animals' habitats could also become possible or some animals would extinguish and new ones appear. Would that be a problem?"

"Freshwater is getting scarce," replied an environmentalist belonging to the group of the climate scientists.

"All those melting glaciers," said the rhetorician using a deep voice and looking surprised. "Surely some of them must contain clean freshwater. Not every bit of the frozen continent is likely to be infected, that would be such a waste, surely, and if that frozen water is a waste, we cannot be too worried about it, I'm afraid."

"If it melts, that water could infect coastlines and human settlements," objected the representatives of the group of the Minorities.

"OK, we won't use it then. Let those glaciers stand for another million or more years and be Mister Uselessness!" In saying this he walked towards the desk of the rhetoricians as if he was about to throw in the towel, but then he suddenly turned around to face All Interests: "Is it true that freshwater is less than three percent of all the water known to us? And that just as little as two percent of freshwater is contained in glaciers, ice and snow while less than one percent comes from the ground and that just a zero-point something comes from the surface of lake and rivers? Such a small quantity, barely over three percent, would certainly require less work to protect than the remaining ninety-seven percent, right?"

"But it's not easy to find groundwater," replied John Delafort, "and if lakes and rivers are polluted, and the glaciers' water is not unconditionally useable, we might be in trouble."

"Aha! Are we facing some difficulty here? On the one hand, we fear the melting of permafrost because of the microbes, bacteria, and viruses that could be released, on the other hand, we might be prevented from using that tiny bit of freshwater they contain because we might not even be able to locate it in the vast icy continent?"

"That freshwater is safe but to get it glaciers would have to melt and what this could mean is not clear yet," replied John.

"Certainly, two percent of the water of the whole frozen continent is a fair bit of fluid, isn't it, and it could keep the earth and humanity safe for long if we only got hold of it, which seems to be difficult due to all sort of problems, I'm told." The rhetorician accompanied the last words with a deep sigh as if wanting to exacerbate the feeling of impotence. "And then I've heard that desalination attempts have polluted the environment and are now a no-go solution." He was accumulating the negatives.

"Let's be parsimonious with water," cried somebody, "let's stop industries that use large quantities of water to produce or to sustain their services."

Close down tourism, hotels, fashion industries, allocate specific quantities of water to families, create houses that can capture rain and use it sustainably within the building, create communities that can manage water grids, stop floating toilets such as cruise ships, forbid fracking and gas exploration. These were some of the suggestions made by several groups.

"Good intentions need to be followed up by good actions," said the deputy-head rhetorician who was interested in achieving solutions based on informed consent, since only they could be implemented by ONO. Silence ensued and it gave everybody time to understand the consequences of the words just uttered. "To protect what we don't have full power over," thundered the rhetorician, signalling to the negotiators that they were entering a new phase of the debate, "seems difficult since to manage things one must first control them, so all this talk about the glaciers and what is stored there seems much too speculative for comfort." He interjected an interval and then said: "It seems that the groundwater sources are far more accessible than others, so it might not be a problem to figure out how to find and protect them."

"We might need to do more than that," intervened Claire, "we might try to imagine the planet earth as a different space from the one we know today, a space linked to the universe rather than an isolated colourful globe, a space where new sources, yes, new water, might one day be found."

"Isn't also that a bit too speculative?" enquired the rhetorician.

Claire offered, "Well, if you think of all that talk about water on Mars that has been around for decades without any evidence at all or about a planet made of a single diamond, if this is not speculation, I don't know what is. The idea that the earth is made of connections between ice and water, rock and sand presupposes connections between central earth and space. Perhaps, there are land corridors or grottos to be found deep in the oceans or even beneath the oceans which might also lead to the deep desert, where I believe different kinds of water and resources are hidden."

"We would like to see some evidence before agreeing on betting only on water," said various representatives of the technology and science groups, who in this issue enjoyed the support of the IBEF Representation.

"We never asked the space agencies around the world to produce evidence. Perhaps this is the reason why they haven't achieved more than cataloguing crazy planets and dead stars. It is not to space but deep into earth that we need to go to understand the life of space," said Claire in an exasperated tone.

"Surely not an easy task," observed the rhetorician, "and I assume that going deep into earth is vastly different from drilling holes in earth?"

"It is," said Claire.

"So how do we do that?"

"Through the oceans."

"So that salty water needs to be protected too?" asked the rhetorician.

"Absolutely, it's our entry point to new discoveries." Claire's strong voice expressed the confidence of her scientific beliefs. "We have explored only a fraction of the oceans and we have mostly focused on marine flora and fauna rather than on their hidden resources."

"But how can that ocean gate be opened and by whom?" asked the rhetorician.

"We are ready to help," said the representatives of Mount View University and the Massachusetts Institute of A.I. "We could create the appropriate complex algorithms and send them out." They looked optimistic. "We will certainly need some new thinking to break through that wall of salty water and find the earth that has remained hidden from us for so long but we are confident that we'll manage it."

"Assume you find new water, what would it be good for?" asked the rhetorician with an inquisitive look.

"Who knows… perhaps we won't need any water on the new earth or perhaps just one drop would be enough to sustain people for a whole life or one drop to prolong life." The person who had just spoken had kept silent during the whole negotiation and seemed to be self-representing. Achilles and his aides did not know who he was nor how he had succeeded in entering the negotiation chamber.

"Sounds too good to be true," said the theologian representing the churches, slightly worried about the earth becoming the centre of everything.

"Look at the way we have approached space," resumed Claire undeterred by his comment, "like blind people entering an unknown room. But the fact is that the sole task of the sun is to dispense warmth to the earth. In my view this shows that there must be a connection between the earth and space that is more productive than we have ever imagined and that the oceans might be the gate that takes us from the earth to space."

"If salty water has this task," declared the rhetorician, "then salty water must be protected, if groundwater is the only water we can drink, then groundwater must be protected, so it seems that the protection of water is best guaranteed by elevating water to the most important resource on earth. Are we ready to agree on this and formalise our consensus?"

Everybody agreed to this proposal.

On having achieved this important result, the rhetorician now opened up a new topic, perhaps to test the strength of the informed consent just reached.

"You are well aware that protection also needs to be linked to enforceable action; this means that we might need to give special status to rivers, lakes, oceans, yes, perhaps to nature as a whole."

"Yes! We want rights to be given to all those entities," declared the representative of First Nations and People.

"We have certainly come a long way since 1972 when Christopher Stone claimed legal status for trees, haven't we?" Here the rhetorician pressed ahead with a difficult line of reasoning. "Are we aware of the consequences of the recent decisions that gave rivers, volcanos, and forests the status of living human entities or the right to be persons?"

"Yes, it's what we want," the representative of Radical Freedom shouted.

"Fine. Then we need to decide one last issue and that is what happens when such entities harm humans out of reasons that have more to do with nature's temper than with human action?"

"We have to accept nature's decisions!" said somebody standing in the space allocated to Young Ecology, a platform of teens who had obtained special permission from Achilles to attend the global negotiation independently.

"How about you teens read a bit about the history of the Enlightenment?" asked the historian representing the Coalition of Humanists. "And perhaps also about some past tragic events such as earthquakes, fires, inundations, the great plague, viruses and many other catastrophes caused by your darling nature when there was no industry polluting anything or human action disturbing the earth?"

"It is certainly problematic," intervened at this point the representative from the group of Atheists, "when human beings are always seen as the culprit and nature as the innocent victim." Some vexed whispers arose from the audience but the atheist would not stop. "And then it's a quick step from nature to God, hey!"

Following this debate, several of the groups attending the negotiation, and some important institutions represented by them, criticised the decisions of various courts to grant legal rights to natural entities. In their views, the courts had given in to radical pressure and some argued that they had been infiltrated by new paganism. The debate showed that there were serious risks in placing nature and humans on the same level. The teens from Young Ecology got a first taste of what it meant to be part of a global society where differing positions had to be negotiated while informed consent must be crafted in cooperation with others.

Summarising the debate, the rhetorician said that the idea that rivers, lakes, and even the oceans could be given full legal rights seemed a quick fix to intricate issues and that it was necessary to develop new thinking. Only so would it be possible to regulate the relationship between nature and humans in meaningful ways. "For the question of rights always also presupposes the question of duties and ultimately of punishment, especially when one entity violates the rights of other entities. But because it seems impossible to imagine how to punish a river, a volcano or the ocean when they burn and inundate human places and peaceful people, it's obvious that these are questions that require a new global negotiation where complex informed consent might have to be developed to address all the issues of nature versus humans."

The rhetorician asked All Interests to support this view and as no one disagreed, he declared the debate concluded and the three major issues discussed during the global negotiation resolved. At this point, the head negotiator, who was responsible for setting the rules of the negotiation, stipulated that the issue of Nature's rights and duties was outside the remit of the present global negotiation and that therefore no conclusive decisions could be made about them. He also said that only Achilles in his role as the director of GAIC and the top negotiator of ONO could host a global negotiation to discuss the rights and duties of non-human agents. Everybody accepted this rule and the granting of legal standing to natural objects was suspended for the time being.

Before calling off the negotiation, ONO allowed the representatives of the Earth Movement to make a public declaration of mea culpa for having stolen the seeds from the vault of Svalbard. At first, they claimed climate defence and argued that their actions had been justified by the inertia of governments to address food shortages. Soon, however, they realised that to stay compliant with the agreements reached during the global negotiation, they would have to drop this claim. Other attendees, particularly the representatives of the Norwegian government, asked for some form of punishment. Achilles, however, reminded everybody that the theft ultimately saved the seeds, for they would by now be lost to humanity had they stayed in the vault. Goodwill was restored in this way and the movement pardoned. Its representatives were given the opportunity to help formulate a manifesto for food that would be discussed at the next global negotiation about agriculture and laboratory food. The negotiation was now coming to an end and after the resolution of some remaining procedural matters, it was officially proclaimed closed. Water had become the earth's resource number one and placed under the protection of ONO and all governments.

Chapter 28

The negotiation had called attention to several issues concerning the future of human society raising questions about humanity's ability to handle new challenges to life on the planet earth. The major difficulty consisted in anticipating risks and opportunities correctly. Informed consent had been reached on some important questions but it seemed difficult to tell how long such consent would last, given the fast pace of change. The hope that a new understanding of the earth could help find solutions to current and future problems was certainly revolutionary. Far from being threatened and in some parts dead, the earth was now seen as a pulsing place, full of vital resources, and what was more amazing was the idea that such resources had remained hidden because of a lack of human imagination. Achilles was proud that ONO had helped the global community clarify not only how to speak about some of today's most controversial issues but also solve them in consensual ways. As the director of GAIC, he was well aware of his responsibility, since the agency had to guarantee that the achieved consensus benefitted everybody. It was also gratifying that ONO had been trusted with the task of implementing informed consent with regard to water. The negotiation had also helped to forge cooperation between groups and communities irrespective of ideologies and ways of life. The negotiators and rhetoricians had done an outstanding job, and Achilles' GAIC was now bearing the fruits. There was one issue, though, that caused personal unhappiness.

Roman had been ill since the return from Svalbard and the destruction of the vault. He lay in the infection ward of a major New York hospital. Achilles had visited him many times but Roman was never able to speak. Often he did not even open his eyes, his tears were the only sign of active life. During a recent visit, Achilles spoke softly into his ear, "Do you remember what happened in the vault when you went back there to retrieve your cameras?" Roman gave no answer, his eyes filled with terror and his body started shaking.

"Don't worry, I'll find out on my own and get you out of this mess," declared Achilles, squeezing Roman's shoulder. One night, Roman would not let go of Achilles' hand. With a dispirited look, he tried to speak but not a single word was intelligible.

"Was there some danger in the vault? Did somebody or something hurt you? How did you get out?"

Roman's look, however, told Achilles that his memory was blank. He seemed to remember only fear and judging from his expression, it was a big fear. Doctors and nurses treating him had to wear protective clothes. Despite the efforts and many tests, Professors Marie-Louise and Justin Goldbrain struggled to understand what was slowly killing Roman. They were the best in the field of unusual infectious diseases but Roman's illness seemed to follow an anomalous script. When Achilles explained to them that his friend had probably fallen into the water that had melted from a glacier, the doctor immediately put Roman under observation, and since that day, he had been kept in hospital out of fear that he might have contracted an unknown virus. The Goldbrains, however, were sceptical about the suggestion, advanced by some colleagues, that the water of the glaciers of the North Pole was infectious. They knew the North Pole very well and disagreed with scientists indiscriminately arguing that the melting ice could unleash old viruses. They supposed that Roman was poisoned before falling into the water, perhaps by spray or some other means. Many experts in the field praised the Goldbrains for having kept Roman alive despite his bad condition. The Goldbrains had developed two cures and had administered one, after which Roman's condition seemed to have worsened. This was the reason why they were now more hesitant about going ahead with the second cure. Achilles was deeply sorry about Roman's condition and felt powerless, a feeling with which he was not very familiar.

One Friday afternoon, Achilles was resting on the couch in his office when Justin Goldbrain called and informed him that Roman's condition was deteriorating and that he would probably die soon. He and his medical team thought that Roman was in extreme pain and that their medication did not seem to give him much relief. The hospital was asking Achilles to inform Roman's family and enquire if they were ready to let him die peacefully. Roman's sister, Loren, who lived in the outskirts of New York, had been in contact with Achilles frequently since Roman's accident. She had been informed about Roman's condition and as a result, she had given Achilles the power of attorney with regard to her brother for she felt emotionally unable to deal with the situation. Achilles thanked Goldbrain and asked him to postpone any decisions regarding Roman until he could visit him at the hospital. Goldbrain assured him that nothing would be done without his approval. After the phone call, Achilles contacted Loren, who cried for the duration of the call, begging Achilles to save her brother, the only relative she had after her son. "Roman," she said, "is the only help I have."

"I will do all I can to get him out of this situation," Achilles said, "I'll be in touch soon. Don't despair, and hugs to little Marvel."

After the phone call, Achilles thought of the photograph that the former director-general had given him as a goodbye gift. He had placed the photograph on the shelf that stood behind his desk on which he kept some of his most important books and objects. He went to the shelf took the photograph and shook it. Instantly, the main picture disintegrated letting appear the little plant and its leaves covered with water droplets. One hundred small leaves covered by one hundred tiny water droplets. Achilles thought that if this was new water, perhaps it could help Roman. He debated with himself whether he had the right to break the frame to collect one drop to save one person, and perhaps risk losing the rest of the water droplets. The glass of the frame was thick and seemingly unbreakable which reminded him of the water jar in the hidden chamber of the vault. "Perhaps it's all a coincidence!" Torn between the choice of getting one water droplet for Roman or saving many droplets for many others, he felt morally blocked. He walked back and forth in his office holding the photograph in his hands and looking at it intently. His mind was pushing him to the limit. *Who knows what this water is really made of.* He thought to himself before returning the picture to the shelf and resolving to never glance at it again.

His sense of sadness was increased by the memory of Roman's pain-stricken face. While he was feeling his lack of power, Achilles heard a noise outside his office door, a kind of rushing caused by soft steps, he then noticed the shadow of somebody walking quickly up the corridor. He knew that only a few people were still in the building, and therefore concluded that it must have been Romeo. He was always one of the last to leave the office on Fridays. Usually, around six, Romeo would come over for a short chat, and on such occasion bring Achilles a cup of Italian hot chocolate. As if Romeo had read his thoughts, he called to say that he would be in Achilles' office in about half an hour. Achilles judged that he would have enough time for a refreshing shower before Romeo's visit. When, after the shower, he returned to his office, he noticed a cup of chocolate on the coffee table. He was at first surprised at not finding Romeo waiting for him, for usually, he came over with a tray on which he also brought a drink for himself. Perhaps Romeo was still too busy to join him.

He took the cup of chocolate and sat on his sofa ready to enjoy it when he noticed a small leaf covered with a drop of water sliding on the surface of his drink. Achilles shook his head in total disbelief but soon recovered himself. He jumped up, went to a filing cabinet and took a small glass container, one of those used in their scientific laboratories, and transferred the leaf with the shining water droplet into it with the help of the little spoon that Romeo left on the saucer. Afterwards, he hastily drank the chocolate, took his coat and device, and walked towards the exit. There he saw Romeo on his way out.

"Thanks for the chocolate!"

"My pleasure," said Romeo in his usual style, "I think your friend looked exceptionally well."

"Which friend?" Achilles asked.

"The one who came to visit you. When I said that I was just about to come up to you with the hot chocolate, he begged me to let him bring it to you. He wanted to surprise you, that's what he said."

"Hm?"

"Come on, that tall guy with that splendid smile," added Romeo.

"Splendid smile?" Achilles' mind ran through all his friends and acquaintances' smiles.

"Did he say his name?"

"Come on, the unusual guy," said Romeo, sounding slightly impatient, adding that after taking the chocolate and moving towards the exit, Achilles' friend had stopped and turned to him said, "Really good to see you again, Romeo."

It can't be Åke, for sure! Achilles thought. He was walking with quick steps towards the elevator. Once there, Angelo came out of his office and asked about his evening plans.

"I'm going to Roman first," said Achilles.

"I'll come with you," said Angelo. Romeo joined them. He had wanted to visit Roman for some time, he said, but could not get a lift to that part of the city, so he was not going to miss this opportunity.

"We need to be fast!" There was apprehension in Achilles' voice.

227

Angelo drove through streets that neither Achilles nor Romeo had ever seen, making them wonder if Angelo had a secret life. They reached the hospital in vastly shorter a time than a cab would have done. Once there, Angelo and Romeo noticed that Achilles set off at a quick pace and concluding that his urgency might originate from some intelligence about Roman's health, they matched his fast tempo. As soon as they entered the infection unit, they saw Martha looking at Roman in anguish. George was also there. Martha, George, and Roman had been friends since early childhood. They went to the same school, the same university, they chose to study science and moved through their various degrees and graduations together. They were friends for life. Martha and George could not imagine themselves without Roman. In quickly entering the room, Achilles had thrown open the door attracting the attention of even poor Roman who was hit by a sudden ray of light from the outside. His status had been upgraded to infection level three and as a result, two glass doors were now separating him from the rest of the world. Achilles looked through the glass doors and noticed that Roman barely moved.

"This afternoon we have tried our second cure," said Mary-Louise Goldbrain, "but unfortunately his condition has not improved, I'm afraid."

"I'm sure you have done everything that is humanly possible under the circumstances, and I am still hopeful that your cure will work," replied Achilles. A sense of helplessness marked the silence that followed his words for it seemed to them that nothing else could be said or done for Roman. It was then that Achilles resumed the talk. "Considering this sad state of affairs, however, I would like to take my leave from him in person before he starts his long journey, and I would also like to say goodbye in the name of his friends and colleagues and pass on a private message from his sister and little nephew." While Achilles was uttering these words, he heard Martha sobbing behind him and noticed Angelo move closer to him.

"Sir," said his assistant, "it's too dangerous." George and Romeo nodded in agreement.

"Open the door, please," said Achilles gently to the Goldbrains.

"No one can enter this room without our permission," replied Justin Goldbrain, his voice calm and resolute. The three nurses and two medical researchers assisting the professors also discouraged Achilles from going to Roman except for one nurse. Judging by her looks, that nurse must have been the youngest member on the medical team. During the past few weeks, she had assisted Roman, and during such time, they had developed a friendship. She now turned her expressive eyes towards Achilles, worried that he might back off in response to Justin Goldbrain's reaction. But she did not know Achilles, she did not know there were reasons why he was ONO's top negotiator. The GAIC's people were also worried but they knew Achilles well enough to know that once he had made a decision nothing could stop him.

"I agree with you, Professor Goldbrain, and thank you for reminding everybody of your authority," said Achilles, "no one should pass those two doors without your permission, except for me!" As he said this, Achilles stretched out his arms and the young nurse, overstepping the chain of command, helped him to put on the hospital's protective gear. The nurse moved fast, she wanted action.

"I give you fifteen minutes," said Professor Goldbrain, "and we are here to help." In saying this, the doctor activated the code that opened the doors.

The first glass door opened, letting Achilles walk through. As he passed it, the door immediately closed behind Achilles' back, while the second door opened. He was now standing next to Roman.

"My friend, I brought something for you and I want you to swallow as soon as I order you to do so," said Achilles to Roman whose look was distant; he was starting to go into a stupor. Achilles moved closer to Roman to block with his body the visual field of the camera placed above the door. He then took out the small glass flacon containing the little leaf with the water droplet and poured it into Roman's mouth.

"What are you doing?" asked Professor Goldbrain from the outside.

Raising his left arm and holding up a little glass bottle Achilles answered, "Giving him some hot chocolate, his favourite drink." Turning to Roman and pressing his hands Achilles finally said, "Have hope!" He waited to see if Roman would respond and to his great surprise, he felt Roman's hand close around his, a weak squeeze but still real. Immediately thereafter, Achilles left the room. He passed the first glass door and was met by the medical staff who, after disinfecting the protective clothes, removed them from Achilles' body. He then exited the second glass door and joined the others. They left the hospital but not before turning a sad look in Roman's direction.

They went out into the cold night. They let themselves be led by Romeo who chose a dining place for them. He always knew how to bridge pain and joy. He was a master of the good

230

life. They were soon seated at a table located in the farthest corner of a good restaurant, enjoying the privacy that the space was giving them. They wanted to speak about Roman and the events that had led to his illness. They had never talked about their last mission to the vault, and suddenly, they sensed that this might be an occasion to do so. The conversation was at first stiff but then all the repressed emotions came out, together with tears and joy. No one really knew what had happened to poor Roman. They discussed many possibilities and concluded that he must have fallen into the waterhole, which by then had enlarged considerably but somehow managed to pull himself out and leave the vault before all his forces were depleted. What they found strange was how difficult it had been for the Goldbrains, whom they truly admired, to stop the illness that was killing him. While they were talking about this the Goldbrains called on Achilles' private device.

"Your friend has regained strength. He's now talking and taking some food." Justin Goldbrain's voice was excited and his joy contagious. Achilles shared the news with his people and everybody in the group applauded, feeling deeply grateful and happy.

"Congratulations, Professors Goldbrain," said Achilles, "we will thank you in a more official way for all your dedication and for the new cure that you have developed."

The rest of the evening passed quietly, and the vault of Svalbard now seemed to be a thing of the past.

When Achilles returned home that night, he noticed that Juanita had shifted some furniture and put his working bags in a different filing cabinet. As he was considering the effects of the change, he suddenly noticed the sealed bag that he had used on the last mission to the Svalbard vault and in which he had put Roman's cameras. On his return to New York, Achilles had taken the bag to the ONO's decontamination unit, which had returned the bag and content to Achilles once cleared. He had taken the bag home for the night but soon forgot about it, probably because the bag had disappeared from his visual field when it fell behind a little piece of furniture in the living room. Driven by a sense of urgency, Achilles now opened the bag by almost tearing apart its zipper. He removed Roman's cameras and noticed that he had labelled them C1 and C2. Achilles went straight to one of his devices and plugged in C1.

At first nothing happened. A few seconds later, however, Achilles saw Roman running towards the camera he had placed on the wall outside the storage hall at the end of the vault's corridor. The video now showed Roman approach the camera. The viewer saw Roman's face in the foreground but the film had also captured the background. To Achilles' total amazement, the wall around the hidden camera was still standing. Suddenly, the door to the hidden chamber flung open letting out a cloud of dust. Roman was unaware of what was happening behind his back until he was seen stretching out his arm to remove the camera, which is when everything turned black. Achilles now plugged in C2. The viewer again saw how Roman was stretching out his arm to remove the camera from one of the walls of the room with the waterhole but then something strange occurred. Somebody or something seemed to grab Roman from behind, then splashes of water became visible which suggested that Roman had fallen or had been thrown into the waterhole. Some shadows became visible but Achilles could not really distinguish what was going on until the shadow of somebody was seen approaching the camera. The light was not strong enough for Achilles to pick up more details but the person collecting Roman's device smiled into the camera, and that smile was the most luminous thing in that vault.

At length he recognised the smile. "Åke," cried Achilles, "you man of infinite resources you are still out there!"

Achilles felt overwhelmed by what had been caught on Roman's cameras. Was it possible that Åke was still in the world? His thoughts suddenly travelled back to the day they went to the vault of Svalbard for the last time. He mentally replayed every single word that was uttered while they were in the vault and he revisited every single move people had made. By now he knew by heart the film he had taken with his body camera. And yet something was escaping him. He went to the window and admired the moon. One of his favourite poems came to mind:

If darkness is around you
Look out for the moon
Her rays give the light
That makes nights bright

He recalled Adam saying that CAs, complex algorithms, can only carry out actions that are infused with human goals because CAs do not have the power of self-motivation, in other words, they always need a human to get into action. Achilles repeated this sentence in his mind and tried to identify what could have allowed Åke to escape. Then, as if the moon had taken pity on him, he understood what might have happened. When Roman went back to collect his cameras, he might have opened up a new field of action for the complex algorithms that were in the vault. Once he reached the door of the hidden chamber, with the intention of collecting camera number one and quit the vault as soon as possible, Roman might have activated the energy that revived Åke. While considering this possibility, Achilles also wondered why he himself or the other members of the team had not been able to rescue Åke when they ran out of the crushing vault.

"Ha, of course!" Achilles slapped his forehead. In escaping the quaking chamber the teams were driven by an instinctive fear but not by a rational goal, which is why their actions could not have reactivated a complex algorithm such as Åke. Roman's action was, however, different. He had expressed an intention to carry out a task, he had a rational goal and so had created the right conditions for CAs to get into action. By wanting to recuperate the cameras, despite the risks that such an action implied, Roman was driven by the energy of a type that he himself and the teams rushing to safety were lacking. All the pieces were now slowly falling into place and it now seemed clear that Roman gave Åke a second chance. When Roman returned to the waterhole room to retrieve camera number two, somebody must have attacked him. The thought that Roman might have clashed with a combative complex algorithm terrified Achilles since he knew by now that these CAs were originally designed to kill humans.

He felt agitated. He went to one of his devices and watched once more the film he had taken with his body camera till he noticed with horror that when the teams were running out of the vault, Melitus was not on the film, to reappear on it again when the film showed Roman emerge stumbling from the ruins of the vault.

Achilles decided to watch again the film recorded by Roman's cameras. He saw Roman race down the tunnel, grab the cameras located across from the storage hall and the thick dust of cold air come out of the vault. Achilles conjectured that the reason why Roman was not stopped at that point was that somebody needed him alive and pursuing a rational goal such as leaving the vault. But Achilles could not imagine which entities were depending, at that precise moment, on Roman's ability to reach the exit. Thinking fervently about the smile recorded on Roman's camera, Achilles concluded that Åke might have saved Roman by pulling him out of the water. Åke must then have carried Roman back to the entrance and helped him get out of the vault. Achilles wondered how many more complex algorithms were in the vault on the day of the mission and if some were combatant CAs.

While this reconstruction brought some relief, it also opened up a new problem; it was now possible to imagine that the waterhole in the room located at the east side of the vault could have functioned as an escape. But who would escape from there or who could have used such a terrifying exit which was leading out of the vault into the vast ocean? Achilles now wondered if Melitus had helped some combative algorithm escape through the hole. This simple thought revived the theory of the waterhole being a gate into the ocean, an issue he had discussed some time earlier with Adam, Martha, George, Olsen, and Neill. Achilles could not decide, however, if the story about the genetically manipulated bacteria eating the vault's floor was still credible.

It did not seem to have survived subsequent developments. In going once more through every moment that preceded the collapse of the vault, Achilles realised that one link was still missing. If complex algorithms need a human with a rational goal to get into action, who did help Åke exit the vault, assuming that Roman must have been unconscious or semiconscious after the attack and therefore unable to embody a rational goal? Or was he still goal-driven? These questions were now uppermost in Achilles' mind. He knew that the answer could help him understand what might have happened after all.

A relentless walking up and down the room did not seem to help him move ahead until suddenly, the whole picture became clear to him. Achilles remembered that Roman was conscious when he collapsed near his feet. In fact, he himself had put the cameras in his hands, so Roman must have had enough motivation to exit the vault and in this way, he must have allowed Åke and possibly other CAs to leave as well. Achilles thought that Roman must have motivated Åke twice: the first time when Roman's goal to get the cameras allowed Åke to exit the hidden chamber and the second time when Roman's goal to quit the waterhole room, no matter how hurt he was, gave Åke the opportunity to exit the vault. But who else had profited from Roman's will? And where was the water jar now? What was all that fuss about using algorithms to protect it if it could be lost so easily? This seemed a more difficult issue to resolve. Algorithms, no matter how complex their design, would still have needed a human will, motivation and capability to carry the jar out of the vault because they themselves can only execute tasks but not intentionally plan them. Assuming the jar was now safe, what or who saved it?

On that front, Achilles had no answers either and he realised that he might never have any. He thought about the little leaf swimming on the surface of his hot chocolate with the water droplet sitting on it. Did Åke put it in there? If not him, who did it? And did it help Roman? He looked out of the window and noticed that the moon had disappeared.

Chapter 29

Roman finally returned to work. Achilles' hope that he could help him reconstruct what had happened in the vault was disappointed for Roman's memory loss was great. Any reference to the vault, no matter how casual, filled his eyes with terror. The psychologist who looked after him believed that the shock had been too strong. Traumas like Roman's, he said, left behind latent dangers since even the smallest detail could cause deep distress. The expert was convinced that to unlock Roman's memory an equally strong shock was needed. The psychologist said that he could trigger the shock artificially and then control its effects. Roman decided to wait before submitting himself to the treatment. For the time being, he was assigned to general tasks such as the classification of files for digital archives. Some suggested that it might be a problem to keep him in that unit but Achilles refused to transfer Roman to another department.

The year was coming to an end. Soon the Christmas festivities would release everybody from work and let people spend time with friends and families. Achilles had a list of presents to buy for his nieces and nephews and for Carlos and Juanita's children. This year, he wanted to start early and savour the gift shopping for his little friends. He had not heard from Olsen or Neill for a while and was wondering if they had moved beyond the past events. Achilles was going to spend Christmas with his family in London and decided to fly to England via Oslo to spend a few days with his friend Bjarne. He wanted to catch up with him after his last bruising visit. He sent a quick message to Bjarne to inform him of his coming. He thought that there might be an opportunity to meet up also with Olsen. The break, though, was still a few weeks away.

One day, while he was looking through the files relating to the vault of Svalbard, Achilles realised that he had neglected to get back to Gwafa Illi to discuss her grandfather and father's mathematical notes. When he finally made contact with her, he discovered that the Queen had gone on a nomadic trip to the middle of the desert. Achilles immediately wondered why she would travel that far considering the recent earthquakes in that part of the Sahara but he then realised that the desert was a familiar place for the Blue People. He left a message for the Queen with her assistant and promised to call again in the new year.

When he arrived at work the following day, Achilles heard the familiar morning chatting of his people. He saw Adam talking to the junior secretaries and the interns, paying a visit to the people in the next office and then to those in the next one. Soon, he would pop in and chat with Achilles. The aromatic scents coming from the café were contributing to people's good mood and it seemed at that moment that nothing could disturb the hard-won peace. Achilles was still affected by what had happened in the vault of Svalbard and felt unhappy about the way the whole case ended. Despite the disappointment about the loss of the water jar, though, he understood that the time had come to focus on procedural matters. The global negotiation on climate change had shown the need to strengthen informed consent with regard to climate, geopolitics, urban and social life, the youth and their expectations, and people's general hopes for a bright future. Achilles spent the day productively working on several important issues, and when he finally checked the time, he realised that the day had passed without him even noticing it. He was still absorbed in his tasks when he saw Roman pass by his office, looking lost.

"Are you alright Roman?" Achilles called out.

"Alright," replied Roman, who stopped so suddenly to catch Achilles by surprise, "but I wonder where the water jar is right now."

"Did it get out of the vault?" Achilles rose from his chair and moved swiftly to where Roman stood.

"Yes!" Roman cried. "Didn't we take it out and put it on the helicopter?" While they were speaking, Martha and George, who were leaving the office, joined them.

"Did we?"

"Yes, it was taken onto the helicopter and was then flown out by the mathematician." Roman was speaking in a mechanical tone, for he had still not completely recovered from his illness.

"Taken to where?"

"To the desert! Don't you remember what the mathematician said… that the water belongs to the sand, that today's people aren't yet ready for it?"

Roman looked at Achilles in total amazement. He could not believe that he, Achilles, had forgotten about the water jar. He turned to Martha and George and noticed stony expressions on their faces. They had moved closer to Achilles and he was now facing them but he would not be intimidated. Roman continued walking toward the main office door, with his back slightly bent, his steps suddenly slow. He reached the exit and left. Achilles turned to Martha and George but no word was uttered by either of them. He grabbed his devices and they left together. New York was enveloped in a grey and humid atmosphere. They went downtown for dinner. They spoke about many things, carefully avoiding the topic that was on their mind. "Let's sleep on it," Achilles finally said, "let's wait till we feel at peace."

They raised their glasses. The bubbling water reminded them of the water jar they had lost in the vault where their friend had lost his mind.

"To friendship!"

Chapter 30

Achilles flew to Oslo on his way to London. He had heard that Neill was also in the Norwegian capital for a few days to meet up with his colleagues before continuing to the Sahara. Preparations were taking place in the Blue City for the official coronation of Gwafa Illi Tin Hinan to Queen of the Tuaregs, now that the mourning period for Queen Mother had come to an end. Once in Oslo, Achilles spent the evening with Bjarne.

"Last time you were here you asked me to keep an eye on the people who came to my hotel," said Bjarne, "and I can tell you that not many strange people came except for a woman who always looked as if she was very busy."

"How would you describe her?"

"Beautiful!"

Achilles laughed at Bjarne's reaction. "You are not helping me a lot," he said.

"She seemed very efficient but always on edge."

"Nationality?"

"When she came to the reception desk she had two passports in a leather pocket, one of which was British, and that was the one she used to register herself as a guest."

"Anything else?"

"Not that I recall… she didn't make a great impression on me but that might be because she didn't seem to have any conversation skills."

"How can you then say that she was efficient?"

"She was always on her devices and on the cellular. One day, she stayed away until very late and when she returned, she seemed exhausted. The following day, which I remember was a Friday, she paid and left one day earlier than her booking. When she came up to the reception desk to settle her account, I noticed a flyer from the Munch Museum next to her briefcase. She placed it carefully into one of her notebooks. Then, smiling at me for the first and last time, she said that treasures must be protected." Bjarne added that soon after she left without a word.

"I asked her if she was unhappy with the service and she replied that mine was one of her favourite hotels and that she would have stayed longer if duties had not interfered and called her away. She didn't mention where she was going."

"Just a busy person, it seems to me," replied Achilles without feeling any alarm.

They continued talking happily about friends and family and planned a short skiing trip before Achilles' departure for London. In the evening, Olsen and Neill came for dinner. They were in good spirits and particularly happy to see Achilles. They were pleased, said Olsen, that the vault of Svalbard was now a thing of the past. But no matter how strongly they set this latter point, they kept returning to the events that happened on the day the vault was crushed. They enquired about Roman's health. Achilles told them about his illness but was quick to add that he was now getting better.

He did not mention the wild exchange he had recently had with him, out of respect for Roman's privacy.

"Thank God, ONO's hospital helicopter was chosen rather than ours," said Olsen at that point, "otherwise he would have died since I don't think that ours was equipped to assist anyone in his conditions."

"What do you mean by ONO's helicopter?" Achilles asked visibly confused. "I thought it was your unit that came with the hospital helicopter."

"So did I," Neill said.

"Well, no," Olsen replied, "it wasn't us who took Doctor Roman to our hospital."

It seems that no one had checked out the full details of that helicopter, and it now appeared that something peculiar had taken place. This information made them immediately suspect that the helicopter might perhaps have been used to transport also the water jar.

"Damn!" Olsen could barely contain his disappointment. "Somebody, there must be somebody who is playing a hit-and-hide game with me," he said, annoyed, "I must find out what happened, especially because that helicopter took off from my base." How was he supposed to communicate this new twist of events to his government? But here, Achilles came to his rescue.

"If the helicopter crew applied for flight permission as an ONO unit, as we can safely assume it did, there would have been no reason for the Norwegian flight authorities to deny permission considering that ONO was in Svalbard on the day of the mission." Achilles' mind was working feverishly.

"The question is," he then remarked, "who did apply for flight permission and who did come to the vault? But the problem is not with you, Colonel Olsen. You and your people did a magnificent job and so did the minister. I think that the issue is more complicated than we might think." Then turning to Neill, Achilles asked for his opinion.

"In hindsight," replied Neill, "what surprised me most was the speed with which Doctor Roman's rescue was carried out. I am also inclined to think that his accident might have disrupted some people's plan, yet those people showed no hesitation in wanting to help Roman. They took him to Longyearbyen, and as I said, even if this meant that they had to alter their plans. If you really think about it, we might not even have spoken about this helicopter if Doctor Roman hadn't required evacuation."

Achilles tapped his forehead. "Silly me, I have with me a copy of the film I took with my 360-degree body camera. Let's watch it again on my device."

They focused on the screen and saw the whole mission happen before their eyes. The teams enter the vault, walk down the tunnel, stand outside the secret chamber, move into the chamber and finally witness the struggle between the algorithms. These scenes were followed by some equally dramatic scenes such as the earthquake, their running out of the vault, the teams standing safely outside, Roman enter the vault again. Achilles' body camera also captured the glacier advancing towards the shore, Roman exiting the vault and collapsing exhausted on the ground. The film continued with Roman lying on the ground and talking to Achilles but the recording did not show Roman placing his cameras in Achilles' hands, because of his proximity to the body camera that he was wearing on that day.

245

Olsen instantly noticed that Melitus was nowhere to be seen when the teams were running out of the vault but that he was back on the film when Roman was laying on the ground. Then the pilot of rescue helicopter prepared for take-off, two crews jumped out, put Roman on a stretcher that had the form of a sealed tube designed to isolate patients from their environment. No one seemed to worry about the sequence of events and even now Achilles and the colonels still found it obvious that Roman had to be isolated. They also noticed, however, that the size of the tube was large enough to contain Roman's body and possibly hide an object of the size of the water jar. As they continued watching the film, they saw that everybody had now moved close to the hospital helicopter to observe the rescue. In a flash, Roman was evacuated. The final scene showed the teams go onto the other helicopters and return to the Longyearbyen base.

Olsen had been on the phone with his aides during the screening of the last sequences of the film. "I've just asked my assistants if a request for special flights had been filed on that day but nope, no such request was ever filed. My people also explained that the helicopter that took Doctor Roman to the base left immediately after the protective tube in which he was lying was removed from the helicopter and taken to the base hospital."

"Do you think the water jar is still in the vault?" Neill asked Achilles.

"Don't know. To be honest, I wonder if we will ever understand what happened."

"Was this the work of some secret service?" Olsen said.

"If a secret service was involved," Neill ventured to say, "it must have been one hell of a first-class service 'cause to carry out such an action without killing anybody and even saving Doctor Roman, showed perfection in action, and today's secret services aren't that perfect anymore."

"Beyond our capability to find out?" Achilles asked.

"Looks like that."

"Hm."

The conversation made Achilles realise that all his attempts to forget the vault of Svalbard had been vain. Reality was that he longed to know what happened to the water jar, yes, he felt that he was in no mood to give it up. After a brief pause, he said, "Let's wait and see if somebody makes a mistake or sends us a hint out of compassion." The irony was not lost on the two colonels.

"More precisely?" Neill seemed to urge some explanation.

At this point, Achilles felt that the time had come for him to share with them his knowledge or at least part of it.

"Somebody helped Roman to get out of the vault," replied Achilles. "Do you remember Adam's conclusions, which I have no reason to doubt, namely that algorithms need humans to get going? That they appropriate the rational goals that motivate human beings? Roman went back into the vault to retrieve two sets of cameras he had placed there. He first went to the storage hall to collect the camera he had hooked up on the opposite wall, he then ran to the room with the waterhole. There too he had put up one camera. In doing so, Roman was pursuing a rational goal, that is, the goal to retrieve his films and get out of the vault as soon as possible. Somebody must have followed him and when he was in the room with the waterhole, he was attacked, and I believe that in that room he was also saved by somebody."

"By whom?" questioned Olsen.

"I believe it was Åke."

"Good old Åke," said the colonel, visibly pleased with the news, "then he's still alive."

"Perhaps Åke was not acting alone. But I cannot imagine who the other person was. Roman's cameras have recorded a struggle but the film is too dark for me to see what is going on. I haven't shown the content to anyone yet because I wanted to give Roman the opportunity to be the first to see his own films, and perhaps get some information from him about what happened in the vault after we left. But now I think it's time to show the films to you, and perhaps you, Colonel Neill, can see what I haven't managed to see so far."

Neill was an expert on infrared light and was skilled at working through dark and bright shadows. Achilles played the films recorded by Roman's cameras, and all three watched the sequences in suspense.

"Good Lord!" cried Neill.

The other two turned to him to see if he could sort out the images. By mainly focusing on the film recorded in the room with the waterhole, Neill said: "There are four shadows clearly visible but at times it seems as if there was another one in the background. Two of the shadows are undoubtedly engaged in a physical struggle, while another shadow is protecting somebody, who might be Doctor Roman. If we go with Adam's theory, this could mean that there must have been three algorithms in the room with the waterhole and all of them had to get out of the crushing vault." Neill paused before continuing with his interpretation of the film.

"Let's assume that Åke was protecting Roman while his friend, who I guess was also a peaceful algorithm, was distracting a combative algorithm by engaging it in a struggle. The combat algorithm seems to grab one of the three, perhaps Doctor Roman, and throw him into the water, hence the water splashing on the film. At this point, however, the images are less clear. What I can see without difficulty, though, is that somebody pulls Roman out of the water, while somebody else gives a hefty shove to one of the shadows, which suddenly disappears from the film. Hereafter, three shadows regroup, with one seemingly being supported by the other two and as a final act somebody collects the cameras that Doctor Roman had hooked up on the wall of the room and gives us a smile."

"Hm, let me go through the situation once more," said Achilles. "If, as Adam once suggested, complex algorithms need humans to carry out their programs by appropriating their goals, it follows that the algorithm that attacked Roman wanted to eliminate the human being who was supplying rational goals to Åke and his friend."

The two colonels did not seem to follow Achilles' train of thought.

"Don't you see what I mean? If the supposedly combative algorithm had killed Roman, then Åke and his friend would have been unable to leave the vault."

"Neither would the third algorithm!" Neill exclaimed.

"Perhaps combat algorithms need humans with a different kind of rational goals to get going…" Achilles intentionally left his sentence suspended.

"Combat humans?" cried Olsen. "Was there a military person in that room who gave a rational goal to the combat algorithm?"

Achilles observed that such a military person would have had no power over Åke because only maths can destroy maths but that person could have harmed Roman and Ake's friend if that friend happened to be a human being. "But of course," he added, "the combative algorithm could have inflicted serious damage to all of them."

Achilles kept speculating. He spoke about Åke's friend: was that friend a human being? Did the friend fight against the military person who was providing the combatant CA with a rational goal? He paused and then struck by a new idea went on. "Listen to this, if Åke's friend was a human being who disabled the military person who influenced the combatant CA, then that combat algorithm was deprived of the person who had provided it with the rational goal to eliminate Roman, Åke and his friend, and then leave the vault."

"I see what you mean," cried Olsen, "If the human person who provided the combat CA with a rational goal was knocked out, then that combat algorithm lost his source of command because algorithms cannot set a goal on their own. But wait a moment, this could mean that he was stuck!"

"Good point," said Neill.

"Unless combatant CAs can appropriate the rational goals of a peaceful complex algorithm," Olsen added.

"I don't think they can," Achilles replied.

"Well, then the combatant CA was unable to leave the vault," said Olsen.

"And it might still be there," observed Neill, "unless somebody helped it to escape."

This latter possibility was deeply unsettling to all three men. Olsen, in particular, realised that this was now a game played closer to home than he had ever imagined.

"So this is where the three ropes came from, it was a military job!" exclaimed Neill. "I now believe the Earth

Movement and its people; they have always affirmed to have blown up the main entrance and entered the vault from there. This was certainly much easier than the use of the ropes, I assure you."

Olsen now realised that he had at least some new evidence to work on, that he was a bit more in control of the past events. They decided to watch once more the film that Achilles had taken with his body camera; in case they had missed some detail. And, indeed, towards the end of the film, they noticed for the first time that there was still one military helicopter on the ground when theirs had lifted. It was part of Olsen's fleet but he could not recall why it was the last to leave.

"What is going on?" Olsen asked Achilles.

Achilles sensed that this question was not solely referring to the events surrounding the Svalbard vault but more generally to the historical moment in which these events were happening. A few minutes' silence followed which was broken by Achilles.

"If that water really exists, this could mean that the planet earth has resources that humans could have never imagined before the discovery of the water jar. That we are now able to discover them, could mean that humanity has crossed a boundary, that we have become more skilful, that we are different from the generations that preceded us. Something similar must have happened to the family of the homo sapiens when they suddenly could do a lot more than all the other hominids had ever done before. Perhaps today's human beings have leapt ahead, have become more agile, are in control of something new, and some of them are already claiming positions. I think that there will be a split between the old and new human being."

"Caused by an epochal clash?" asked Neill.

"Not in biblical terms," replied Achilles, before adding: "we are all walking along the same path but some people are faster than others. Let's try to catch up and move one step ahead of them."

The colonels felt all the force of the compliment.

"We will help you to catch up," said Neill, "but to be one step ahead is something for you, Achilles, we don't have the sensibility and skills to tame that intelligence ahead of us. But we can help you, protect you, safeguard consensus, and help enforce informed consent if and whenever necessary. We can anticipate the physical risks and dangers and create safe ways for the people on that path."

They rose and shook hands. Achilles needed them to create and implement informed consent, and they needed his knowledge to be able to reform their own profession and add new skills, so they could keep walking on that path and work for peace.

Chapter 31

Achilles made a video call to Romeo. He found him preparing dinner for a group of friends that included Roman, the young nurse Mary, Roman's sister Loren and her boy, Marvel, and some other people unknown to Achilles. Romeo and Achilles chatted jovially about food and vacation plans. Before ending the conversation, Achilles asked for Roman. Soon he had him on the screen talking about trying to dissolve that piece of blocked memory that was separating past and present.

"I want to be as I was before…"

"Hm, might not be easy."

"Why?"

"Are not our experiences supposed to change us?"

"Can we become worse than we were?"

"Possibly. But usually, people learn from what they experience and draw positive conclusions."

"I have lost a piece of my memory. I only remember entering the vault and exiting it." Roman seemed to struggle with containing his emotions when he uttered these words. He mentioned that his psychologist had again suggested a virtual reconstruction of the events that happened in the vault. According to the psychologist, his memory has created a block that is preventing him from seeing selected events. Roman asked Achilles for his opinion.

"Do you want to see what could unleash great pain?"

"If that is the only way to get my memory back, then, yes, I would."

"Memories can be cruel," Achilles replied. He noticed apprehension in Roman's eyes.

"Why don't we let things take their natural turn," Achilles said at this point, "perhaps one day your memory will unblock itself without the use of external stratagems. If say, in six months nothing happens, we might want to start considering trauma therapy and perhaps after a little while, start preparing for it. What do you think?" The plural pronoun reassured Roman that he was not alone, that he had friends.

"Sounds good to me," he then replied relieved, "yes let's do that."

They continued talking about various things related to Roman's vacation, and then Achilles took his leave from the whole group. He knew that as long as Roman was with Romeo, he would be fine.

A message came in on his private device. It was Adam informing him that he was about to leave and that he would be in touch soon. Adam was going to the Blue City for the coronation of Gwafa Illi Tin Hinan. Adam had wanted Achilles to accompany him but he had declined. It was Adam's opportunity to meet with several government representatives as the new ONO director-general and to forge alliances or learn where opposition grew, without Achilles' influence. Adam was at first reluctant to go alone but when Achilles suggested that he should take Meher with him and also invite Angelo, Martha, George, and the junior secretaries,

Adam immediately agreed. They had worked hard over the past months and deserved a break. For Adam, it would be an occasion to be with them outside their usual working space.

Achilles received another message on his work device, this time from George and Martha informing him that during their stay in the Blue City they would meet with some colleagues, and they included his friends, Claire and John, with whom they would go on a scientific tour to the desert. Then the two junior secretaries, Lucillo and Parys sent a video message to tell him that they were about to fly out with Adam and Meher and meet Annabelle in the Blue City. They also mentioned that in two days' time, they would attend a concert in the desert at which the band *Save the Earth* was also going to perform. *There you go!* thought Achilles.

Angelo also wrote to him. "Sir, I'm about to attend the coronation of Gwafa Illi Tin Hinan, the future Queen of North Africa. It'll be an historical celebration." Achilles smiled at Angelo's way of expressing himself since he only considered his trip to the Blue City from a monarchic perspective. Achilles knew that the future Queen would make Angelo feel at home.

A separate video message now came in from Annabelle. She looked happy when she recounted her meeting with Gwafa Illi during which she informed the Queen about the plant and water that she had found in the desert and brought to ONO. Annabelle also told him that Gwafa Illi had enquired if Achilles was aware of the finding and of Annabelle's disclosure to her, and that when she, Annabelle, confirmed that he, Achilles, was aware and supported her disclosure, Gwafa Illi smiled and thanked her for her information. In parting, the Queen pressed her hands and wished her a happy stay in the Blue City.

Achilles walked to the window. The night was bright and Oslo's Nordic light captivating. Shortly, he would go to the airport and fly to London. He suddenly realised that the year was going to be over in just eight days. *Was the New Year going to be as memorable as the old one?*

Both ONO and GAIC had accomplished a lot and there were good reasons to be satisfied. He only wished to know the whereabouts of the water jar and if it really contained a new kind of special water. He realised, though, that even if he had the opportunity to see the water jar again, he would not be able to say anything about the quality of the water; but he would certainly feel relieved to know that the water jar was safe.

He sensed that the whole story of the water jar was to remain a mystery and the problem was that it was still distracting him. He sighed and turned to the photograph that the former director-general had given him as a present on his departing day. For some strange reasons he had put it in his travel bag. He looked at it and saw his people in the foreground, lively, smiling, and happily chatting. Then he shook the photograph and the hidden background came to the fore. Achilles instantly noticed that one of the tiny leaves had gone. He felt his heart leap ahead. As he was looking at the spot with the missing leaf, he heard a soft sound come through from his classified device. He saw "access requested" in flashing red. The people who had exclusive access to his device need not to ask for permission to speak with him which made him conclude that whoever was now trying to get through to him had not clearance. The IT department had explained to him the risk of granting access to unknown requesters, so he instantly denied access and to protect his classified device, he blocked the caller. Two minutes later, an "access requested" appeared on his work device. This time he granted access. At first, nothing happened but then suddenly and instantly, the water jar appeared on the screen, as beautiful as ever. Held against the light of the sun, it had content that shone like a liquid gem. A message followed: *Happy New Year, Achilles.*